I've travelled the world twice over,
Met the famous: saints and sinners,
Poets and artists, kings and queens,
Old stars and hopeful beginners,
I've been where no-one's been before,
Learned secrets from writers and cooks
All with one library ticket
To the wonderful world of books.

# LION IN THE EVENING

British soldiers are trapped in a remote, dusty town in East Africa during World War I. German troops have breached the perimeter. The lives of the troops and wounded depend on two men and a railway line. Richard Kendon, a young American engineer caught up in a war that has nothing to do with him, finds himself working against time to complete the line and give the troops their only possible escape route. But two man-eating lions are killing the Indian labourers—can the railroad be finished in time?

# ALAN SCHOLEFIELD

# LION IN THE EVENING

*Complete and Unabridged*

# ULVERSCROFT
*Leicester*

First published 1974 by
William Heinemann Ltd., London

First Large Print Edition
published September 1980
by arrangement with
William Heinemann Ltd.
London
and
William Morrow & Co., Inc.
New York

British Library CIP Data

Scholefield, Alan
  Lion in the evening. — Large print ed.
  (Ulverscroft large print series: adventure,
    suspense)
  I. Title
  823'.9'1F      PR9369.3.S3L/

  ISBN 0-7089-0515-3

Published by
F. A. Thorpe (Publishing) Ltd.
Anstey, Leicestershire
Printed in England

*For Charles Pick*

# PROLOGUE

THE lion lay in the shadows of the railway cutting and watched the man. There was no moon but the starlight made the scene almost as bright as day to the huge pupils of the lion's eyes. The man could not see well, and to help him he used a candle cupped in a brown paper bag. This supplied him with just enough light to work by.

The man's name was Zietsmann, Lieut. Walter Zietsmann of the German East African Protective Force. He was twenty-six years old and he was fixing a charge of high explosive to one of the fish plates of the railway line. The year was 1916: Britain and Germany were at war. The railway line, which ran from Mombasa to Lake Victoria through the heart of British East Africa, was like a great artery: damage it permanently and the country would bleed to death.

The lion was much older in feline terms than Lieut. Zietsmann was in human. He was in great pain; there was pain in his mouth and in the pads of his front paws: nowadays he was never without pain. He was also hungry.

He had tried, and failed, to kill a wildebeeste three days before and had then been lucky enough to find the remains of a British soldier who had died of dysentery and whose body had been dug up by jackals. But that had been seventy-two hours ago.

Lieut. Zietsmann began to pay out the quick-burning fuse, backing away from the railway tracks as he did so. The movement was like a trigger to the lion.

It did not spring or bound, but seemed to flow over the ground, keeping very low. Twenty yards from the man it let out a grating snarl. Lieut. Zietsmann dropped the fuse and began to turn, then changed his mind and swung back to run. He had only taken a single step when the lion was on him. He felt the tearing weight crash into his back, felt the forepaws lock around his throat, felt the agony as the jaws closed on his shoulder. And that was all he felt for, although he did not die at once, all feeling vanished.

The lion picked him up and carried him back into the shadows of the cutting. There was a blurred yellow movement above, and another lion, also a male, but just coming into his full strength, sprang down to join him. The old lion dropped the body and stood over it, growling far back in his throat. The younger animal kept five paces away.

Zietsmann opened his eyes for the last time. Above him he saw the lion and struck feebly at it with his undamaged arm. The animal jerked back, snarling, and then, like a kitten skipping to a feather, it jumped forward. Zietsmann gave a single cry but was dead before his own ears heard it.

The lion began to feed. The younger animal edged nearer, lay down, got up, began nervously circling the food, kept back only by the snarls and growls of its companion: there was not a great deal of Lieut. Zietsmann to feed two lions.

Without warning, there was an explosion farther up the line. And then another. The lion stopped feeding. Both animals stood near what was left of the body. There was a third explosion then the harsh sound of heavy boots on clinkers. The young lion leapt up the side of the cutting.

"Walter," a voice called softly. "Walter, wo bist du?"

The old lion moved away from the body. The beam of a lantern began to flicker over the cutting walls. The lion melted into the shadows.

3

"Walter!" the voice cried. "Lieber Gott! Walter!"

The old lion loped along the railbed. The sounds of shouting grew fainter and finally ceased. About midnight the two animals drank from a pool that had formed beneath a leaky water tower, then they went on, travelling slowly, always keeping to the railway, the source of food.

# 1

WHEN Richard Kendon woke, the early sun was already making the inside of his tent a sweat-box. He lay under the mosquito net on the damp sheets, unwilling to rise, unwilling to remain. Every morning he experienced this feeling of slight dread without immediately being able to identify it. Then abruptly it broke on him: the schedule. The schedule for this section of the Kisimi spur line, which had branched away from the main Mombasa-Lake Victoria railway far to the south-east, called for him to key a mile of steel a day, but for the past three weeks he had been slipping farther and farther behind. According to the schedule, the three viaducts should have been finished, yet the third was hardly begun. Around him he could hear the unmistakable sounds of a big railway construction camp coming to grips with the new day. He sat up on the narrow camp bed and fumbled in his military chest for quinine tablets. They said if you took quinine over a long period it made you deaf.

"Luke!"

"Bwana?"

"Shaving water."

He leant from the cot, shook out his socks and boots in case of scorpions, then began to dress. As he did so he noticed that his bush-shirt needed repair. So did his khaki shorts—"Bombay bloomers", as the Superintendent of Works called them. They were part of the uniform of the settler population of British East Africa. Some varied the monotony of their dress with python or leopard-skin hat-bands. Kendon wore a red and green paisley-patterned bandana knotted around his throat: it gave a splash of colour to an otherwise monochrome effect.

Luke gave him his breakfast under his usual tree. He could see Jemadar Ragbir Singh hovering on the edge of his vision. He ate his way through a plateful of bacon and eggs, then sat back with his second cup of tea. His eyes rose to the Escarpment. They did so every morning. The great grey slab of forest-covered mountain rose out of the flat plain like a huge wave, gently on this side, more sharply on the other. There was no way around it for a hundred miles in either direction. On its far side, less than fifteen miles from Railhead by the shortest route, lay Lake Kisimi and on its farther shore the town of Kisimi. This morning, as on many mornings, the summit of the Escarpment was hidden in swirling mist.

He had been staring at it for months. Each few weeks, as Railhead was moved forward, the great ridge came closer, so that what had once been a dark haze near the summit gradually strengthened until it became a forest; soon he would be able to see individual trees. The Escarpment lay across his path like some great blight. If he had ever known its native name, he had forgotten it. To Kendon it was the Escarpment, not ever the 'scarp' as the Superintendent had called it. He remembered his first arrival at Railhead, then nearly eighty miles to the south-east, when he had replaced Collins, now dead of fever. The Escarpment had only been a smudge on the horizon then. He had hardly noticed it; he had been too shocked by his surroundings. He had not lived a coddled life. He came from a family of engineers. His father had been a mining engineer in Colorado, his grandfather on his mother's side had been a ship's engineer, born and bred in Glasgow. Kendon himself, since leaving college with a civil engineering degree, had been part of that freemasonry of American engineers who could be found from Nicaragua to New Zealand, drilling for oil, building bridges, dams, roads and railways. He specialized in railways. He had worked on tracks in Mexico and Bolivia, in crushing heat and the bitter cold of the *altiplano*, but he had never encountered anything like the scrub desert of British East Africa and nothing he had ever read about Africa had prepared him for its reality. He had come up from Nairobi with Mr. Campbell, the Superintendent, and when they had reached Railhead—indistinguishable from the present camp—he had said, "Not the most salubrious spot on earth. But you'll get used to it."

Kendon had stared at the wait-a-bit thorn, a tangled thicket of green leaves and yellow hooks, the low stunted trees, the ridges of reddish, heat-blistered rock. Everything had a ghastly, sun-stricken look. The only living things he saw were lizards flicking in and out of the rock crevices. At that moment he regretted the impulse which had brought him to Africa.

"Don't try to tame it," the Superintendent had said. "If you do, it'll destroy you."

Kendon had got used to it. He had lived in it now for more than six months and no longer saw it with the freshness of that first encounter. He knew it a great deal better. The *nyika*, it was called. He had twice ventured into the thickets, once after shooting a guinea fowl, the second pursuing a wounded wart-hog. Both times he had been badly scratched and had had to be released from the hookthorns which fastened into his clothes and held him immobile. Since then he had kept to the open spaces.

In a sense the railway, too, was a prisoner of the bush. Once the steel began to climb the Escarpment they would be in different country, wooded but without thorn, the air would be clearer, cooler, they would be able to breathe again. But the Escarpment held its own problems. The tracks were to follow the old slaving route to the top of the pass, climbing and twisting across the face of the mountain, crossing three narrow clefts. These clefts, which were wide but not high, meant three viaducts, the longest of which would have eight piers. Work had been going on for months and two were completed. But the third and largest was hardly begun. Although they had dug deeper than on the two previous viaducts, they had still not found a good rock foundation.

The schedule. . . . Time was not so much slipping as rushing away.

"We're at war," the Superintendent had said. "The future of the Colony might depend on this railway."

Kendon lingered a few seconds longer but the day was pressing on, the schedule unfulfilled. He put down his cup and strode towards the summit of a rise which would place him above Railhead Camp. He was a tall man in his early thirties with long loose limbs and sandy hair and deep brown eyes that gave an intense cast to his features, as though there was something unexpected, something hidden behind them.

His walk was deceptive. It appeared to be casual, but Jemadar Singh, who had waited patiently while the sahib finished his food, had to hurry to keep up. As they climbed the slope the Jemadar kept up a sing-song patter with much consulting of his notebook: ". . . new cases fever No. 1 camp, two . . . new cases fever No. 2 camp, nil . . . new cases dysentery (he pronounced it deesenterri) No. 1 camp, one . . . No. 2 camp, one . . . one case sore eyes No. 1 camp, two cases. . . ."

"Anything serious?"

The Jemadar looked up, confused. The

daily liturgy irritated Kendon by its remorseless attention to detail, but it was his own fault. He had asked the Jemadar to be as meticulous as possible. "I'm sorry. Carry on."

"Two cases drunkenness No. 1 camp . . ."

"Where'd they get it?"

For a second the Jemadar's mind saw Karim Ram, then the picture was erased.

"Nobody knowing, sahib."

"Tell the Clerk of Works to dock them three rupees each."

The Jemadar made a note in his book. ". . . One tent burn down No. 1 camp, two goats stolen . . ."

And so it went, the venalities and infirmities of four hundred male human beings isolated in two camps in the middle of Africa, far from their native heaths. At first Kendon had been surprised that the labour was all Indian, but he had discovered that the Mombasa-Lake Victoria railway from which they were taking this branch line, had been built fifteen years before by Indian indentured labour, by many of the very people who had been recruited to the present task. The local Masai and Nandi tribesmen would have considered such work beneath them.

11

". . . stone mason from No. 1 camp bitten by snake . . ."

"Anyone see it?"

"Four people seeing snake, sahib, but they not knowing what kind. Two saying it thick and short, two saying it long and thin."

Kendon glanced at his watch. Two trains reached them from Nairobi each day. The first, early in the morning, was the materiel-train, carrying the steel, the fish plates and fish bolts, the sleepers. The second came in the evening with the daily water and food supplies. "Better get him on the early train to Nairobi. And the fever and dysentery cases." When he had first arrived there had been a doctor, but he had been recruited by the Army and now all serious cases had to be returned to Nairobi for treatment.

"The *bhisti* from No. 1 camp gone missing," the Jemadar continued.

"What do you mean, gone missing?"

"He not there, sahib."

"Which one?" Kendon asked, trying to remember which water carriers worked at No. 1 camp."

"The lame one, sahib. He calling himself Ali."

"Didn't we have trouble with him before?"

"Drunk, sahib."

"Well, he'll turn up. Three rupees." The Jemadar noted the fine.

Kendon was standing on top of the rise and from it he could look down on No. 1 camp. The tents were spread out along the track and on the slope of the opposite rise, wherever there was a gap in the *nyika*. There was activity everywhere: the morning works train was being unloaded and its engine was already on the loop. In an hour it would return to Nairobi. Away to his left he could see the white tents of No. 2 camp at the base of the Escarpment. Nearer he could make out tiny figures manhandling sleepers and, even closer, the plate-laying gangs. It was like watching the organized confusion of a colony of ants.

Since his assistant, Willard, had gone down with blackwater fever and had been removed to Mombasa, Kendon had been in sole charge of the two camps. Several times he had asked about Willard's replacement and on each occasion had been told there was a war on.

It was time to go to No. 2 camp. He hurried down the slope. Immediately the breeze vanished and the stifling heat of the *nyika* closed in. The coolies swarmed around him.

13

Everything was hot. Everywhere was noise. It was the noise of metal upon metal, iron upon steel. Even the sleepers, now too hot to touch, were made of metal because white ants destroyed the wooden ones.

He climbed aboard the trolley which he used as a flivver to commute between the two camps and seated himself in the old basket chair that had been strapped on to the platform. Two coolies began to work the hand levers. As the trolley picked up speed he felt the sweat begin to dry again.

Half-way between the camps he saw a small group of coolies standing by the track. One looked up as he heard the clack-clack of the trolley and started to run towards it, shouting "Sahib! Sahib!" The trolley stopped. The knot of coolies stood facing Kendon. At first he thought they looked sullen, almost mutinous, then he saw that their eyes were afraid. He jumped off the trolley and the group opened. The soft earth of the railbed was badly cut up. He looked more closely and saw morsels of gristle and bone and bits of bloodstained cotton. A little farther on he saw a skull, jaws and some of the larger human bones.

"There, sahib!"

14

There was a portion of a man's palm with two fingers attached. On one was a silver ring.

"It is the *bhisti*, sahib. It is Ali's ring."

Less than sixty yards away and deep in the *nyika* lay the two lions. Both were tired after their journey from the main line. The older one, still in great pain, was half awake. The younger one fully so. If the smell of man grew stronger, if the voices grew louder, the lions would move. Until then their cover was good enough.

# 2

ON the afternoon of the same day on which the *bhisti's* remains were found, Margaret Storey was making her way down the little, dusty main street of Kisimi. She had been lying down and she could still feel the sweat under her arms and in the V of her neck. Although she had not slept, the heat had made her thick-headed.

The town was dead. Later there would be a breeze from the lake and the streets would come alive but now nothing stirred in the wet heat. She walked in the shade of a straggling line of jacaranda trees, fanning herself with a paper fan and using a parasol to keep off the errant sun rays that broke through the foliage. Before the war the streets, even at this time, would have been lively: there would have been the usual knot of tribesmen talking and shouting to each other; the delivery boys slowly pedalling their bicycles. She had never thought much about them before, now she missed the vitality they had brought. She passed the bank. Often she would have met

Eric Loader or Ralph Sissons coming from its dark interior and one or the other might have taken her for a glass of lemonade at the Britannia Restaurant. It had helped to break up the day.

Both were gone now, like the black people, into the Army. There was a rumour that Ralph had won a medal but one couldn't be sure. The black soldiers, the *askaris* as they were called, were also said to be doing great things. It was odd: people had said they were impossible to train for anything; now the same people were saying what good soldiers they made.

But that was the only difference the war seemed to have made to Kisimi. When she was by herself it was often difficult to believe there was a war at all, yet the moment people got together the talk was about nothing else. She was no expert but she had picked up enough in conversation and read enough in the newspapers that came through from Mombasa to know that things were not going well for the British in Africa. The German East African forces were led by General von Lettow-Vorbeck. Although the German Army was small and poorly armed, the British were unable to damage it. Her father had described the British generals as incompetent old women and she had heard that one general, at least, was an alcoholic.

At the beginning of hostilities the British High Command in East Africa had considered that it would take only a few weeks to crush the neighbouring German colony. They had launched an attack on the German East African port of Tanga that had turned into one of British history's greatest defeats. Now, after nearly two years, they knew what any British settler could have told them: the Germans were just as tough, just as resourceful as they were themselves, possibly more so.

For the Empire forces, the war had turned into a ghastly copy of the Boer War. Von Lettow-Vorbeck led them deeper and deeper into the wilderness, blowing up their lines of communication, ambushing them almost at will, never fighting a pitched battle, letting malaria and blackwater and dysentery do what his 1873 rifles were incapable of doing.

There was no front line as such, everything was fluid. It was the sort of warfare for which the Empire forces were tactically unfitted. But the latest rumour to reach Kisimi was that a contingent of South Africans would soon arrive. Their General Smuts would take overall command and this was regarded in Kisimi as a hopeful sign, since he was one of the Boer commanders who had led the British such a costly dance fourteen years before.

She walked on past the Britannia and stopped at the post office. "Afternoon, Mr. Mackenzie," she said, putting her head around the door. The heat in the corrugated-iron building was dreadful.

"Afternoon, Miss Storey. Yes, post's in at last. I'm on yours now. How's the Colonel?"

"Not too badly, thank you."

"Look at this!" He held up an envelope. "From the King of Sweden, it says."

"Shall I call back?"

"Give me a few minutes. Is it all right if I have the stamps?"

"Of course, only . . . last time you tore one of the letters. Father gets . . ."

"Oh, dear! Tell him how sorry I am. I'll take extra care." He pushed the spectacles back on his sweating forehead.

She went to the edge of the lake. The road petered out. Half a dozen small ferry boats were pulled up on the mud. Another lay in the shallows, its boards stove in. Small tilapia were swimming in and out. Someone had

19

flung the wheel of a bullock cart into the clear water and there were a number of rusty tins. On the far side of the lake the Escarpment rose from the plain. The double barrier of water and mountain made her feel even more cut off from the outside world than usual. The arrival of the post should have broken this feeling of isolation but it hadn't. Often it signalled one of her father's bad days.

After a few moments the glare of the lake was too much for her and she walked into the "public gardens"—a few square yards of green turf and shade—and sat down on a bench in front of the monument. There was no one about, though usually, at any time of the day, there would be one or two tribesmen staring at the monument. It was a traction engine of gleaming brass and green paint, fly wheels and pistons and great painted wheels. To the tribesmen, it was an object of infinite wonder, standing there on its stone plinth. On one side it bore the legend, "John Fowler & Co., Leeds", and underneath, "Presented to the citizens of Kisimi by Colonel Frederick Seaton Storey."

"Good afternoon, Margaret." Harry Goodman, the Police Inspector, stood at the end of the bench, towering above her, his face redder than ever. With him was a corporal holding a rifle, and four prisoners from the gaol in the police compound.

"Get cracking!" Goodman said. The corporal waved his rifle and the prisoners, each carrying a bottle of polish and a rag, swarmed over the traction engine, cleaning brass and paintwork. "Lovely thing, isn't she?" he said.

When Margaret had first come to Kisimi more than eight years ago he had paid her exaggerated court. She had been nineteen and he a divorced man nearly twenty years older. She had gone to tea with him once or twice at the Britannia Restaurant and he had asked her to marry him. When she refused there had been an ugly scene in the dark garden of her house. After that she had not seen him for months. When they did meet again he carried on as though nothing had happened. She had never told her father.

"How's the Colonel?" he asked. "Didn't see him at the Club last night." He had a habit of standing to attention and bending forward from the waist when he addressed her.

"No. He was busy."

"He's a man of vision!" he said, as though trying to impress her with his gravity, then spoiling the effect by turning and shouting, "Come on, Corporal! Get those so-and-so's working! We're not here to sit on our thumbs!" The traction engine shone so much in the sunshine that the reflection hurt her eyes.

To Kisimi, it was an object of pride. Rumour had it that it had been used in the Boer War as an armoured road locomotive and had then been brought here by sea, land, river and lake to haul diamond-bearing ore. But there had been no diamonds and it had ended up, some years later, hauling building sand and gravel for Colonel Storey. When he had given up his sand pit the traction engine had stood in the garden, growing rusty and weatherbeaten, until Goodman had taken an interest in it. He had got it to work and had then suggested it be given to the town. It was Kisimi's one historical document. Goodman allowed no one else to look after it. Many people found it romantic; to Margaret it was a lump of metal that reminded her too vividly of an unhappy time.

She rose. "I must be going."

He touched his cap in salute. "Time flies! You and the Colonel must come over one evening for coffee and a chat."

"I'll ask him."

"Make it soon. We're going to be busy when the Army gets here."

She went back to the post office and collected the bulky pouch of letters. She could no longer postpone her last call.

She crossed the street and went down what began as a wide road but deteriorated into a track. She walked carefully, avoiding the potholes. After a few yards the buildings degenerated into one-roomed shacks shaded by mango trees. From the main street it was only a matter of minutes before she found herself on the outskirts of the town. Mr. Patel's was the last shop, the last building, before the bush closed in. It lay off the road but was easily found by the paths which converged upon it from all directions. Thousands of bare feet had worked the black-cotton soil into hard-baked trails. The sign outside the shop read, "B. K. Patel. General Dealer". She entered the dim building and smelt burning joss-sticks. She was relieved to find herself the only customer.

The bead curtain at the back of the shop opened and Mr. Patel came into the room. For a moment she saw through to the rear. A woman was bending over a table and there was a smell of ground cardamom, turmeric and coriander.

"Welcome, welcome," Patel said, moving towards her. His mouth smiled but his eyes remained uncommitted.

"Hello, Mr. Patel."

"Very hot today. Very hot." He was a tall, thin Hindu with prominent cheekbones and steel-rimmed glasses. "How is the Colonel?"

"He's well, thank you."

"Good. Good. And what can I do for you?"

She longed to say: *It's all right, I promise you'll get paid.* But she couldn't. And she knew that Mr. Patel knew she couldn't. It would so reverse established roles as to open a deep wound in their relationship. The game of pretence had to be played out: she would not acknowledge that they were in his debt and that they bought groceries only by his grace; he would not admit that they were not doing him a favour by simply coming into his shop. When she had bought the groceries at Tucker's on the main street all important communications had been committed to paper and arrived through the post. This enabled Mr. Tucker to remain friendly in person while cutting off their credit in a coolly-phrased letter. The letter seemed to come not so much from him as from some machine that looked after his interests. Mr. Patel did not send bills nor write letters. His shop dealt mainly in one- or two-rupee sales to tribesmen. There was no machine looking after his interests; everything was personal, face to face.

He had been both pleased and suspicious when Miss Storey had come to his emporium: pleased because the Storeys were the first white family to support him, suspicious because he could not fathom why they had come. When the reason became apparent he told himself that even if they couldn't pay, they were a good advertisement. Other white families might follow, since his prices were lower than Tucker's.

Nothing of the kind had happened. But her father was a colonel and it was said that the Army was coming to Kisimi. Things might change, one never knew.

"Half a pound of tea . . . two loaves of bread . . . a tin of sardines . . . a tin of butter . . . two pounds of rice . . ."

Patel wrote it down in his book. At first she had asked him, "Would you put that down in the book, please." Now he anticipated her. As she looked up at the shelves, he watched her. She was small and dark and he supposed white people might find her pretty.

"... Two tins of sausages ... and a packet of Sunlight soap ..."

She was exhausted when she reached home. She shuddered at the very prospect of entering the store again, yet she knew she would need something tomorrow or the following day ... and the day after that ...

As the afternoon died, she and her father sat on the screened-in porch. Slowly the breeze from the lake crept across the baking earth towards them.

"Shall I light the lamp, father?"

He did not look up from the letters on the card-table. "If you wish it."

In the language in which their relationship was conducted, this meant *I do not wish it*. She watched him over her mending. He had been heavily muscled, but now the muscles had gone. Years of harsh African sun had left the loose skin of his face and neck like crushed leather. Once he had been a big man, but now he seemed to have fallen in on himself as an old building falls in. Much of the deterioration had occurred after his accident but even before, as a little girl, she had known that his skin was different from other

26

people's. It was hard and rough, and his hands were cut and calloused. Yet he was not entirely a product of the bush. He wore his khaki with a certain elegance. His soft buckskin shoes were cut on the South African pattern, with high throats, his bush-shirt was more green than khaki, and he wore a yellow silk scarf at his throat. His iron-grey hair was well brushed and his moustache severely clipped.

He had been working on his letters for more than an hour. There were nearly twenty and each had to be entered in his book, marked with the date, filed and cross-indexed. At last he was done. He sat back and began to fill his pipe. For a long time he sat staring out at the mango trees in the garden. She watched him, then she said, "I saw Harry Goodman this afternoon. He wants us to have coffee and a chat some time."

He appeared not to have heard.

"He says he thinks you've got great vision."

When he did not reply she went on with her mending for a minute then, as though fearing a vacuum, said quickly, "I hear Ralph Sissons has won a medal for gallantry."

Her father removed his pipe and said,

"The postal service is atrocious!" He spoke as he might have done to a stranger. "God knows, I don't expect miracles. I realize the letters from Europe and America must take slightly longer because of the war, but some of these—" He flicked the pile in front of him, "—have taken nearly three weeks from Mombasa."

"That's one thing the railway will change when it gets here," she said.

"So you keep telling me. And what of the other things it'll change? We'll have all the yahoos from the coast up here in no time."

"Why should anyone come *here*, father?"

"Why? Good God, why does anyone go anywhere? I tell you, they'll be up here in their droves, poking about. And they'll disturb the blacks."

As he took up his pipe again she saw a tremor in his hands and regretted the idle remark she'd made about the railway. Anything that encroached on what he called the "old Africa" was to be fought and if there was no possibility of winning, to be ignored. The railway was anathema to him.

"Anyway, when we get the sanctuary they can do what they damn well please. We'll be well out of it. We'll be in the bush again.

Deep in it. The only place for a man."

He spoke, she thought, as though to reassure himself that he would return to the life he had known; that Kisimi was an interlude which would come to an end. His plan for a game sanctuary had become an obsession. Through it, he would be able to get back to the bush without having to kill animals, without ever having to pull the trigger of a rifle again. But she was certain of one thing: she would rather die, rather marry Harry Goodman than go back into the "old Africa" with her father.

The short twilight was deepening and she took the opportunity of breaking his train of thought by fussing with the lamp. When the wick was burning evenly she settled down once more to her work. Her father still sat stiffly in his chair.

"It's incredible," he said, once more addressing a stranger. "You offer people the chance of doing something . . ." His voice faded. "I can't fathom it. D'you think they simply don't *care*? I mean—" he picked up a letter "—look at this ass. Supposed to be a church leader. He says don't I think mankind more important just now than animals. As though the two things were incompatible."

He began the complicated process of getting out of his chair, first raising himself on his arms, then shifting his weight from his damaged hip, then gripping his stick. Margaret watched with a mixture of pity and irritation. "Let me get it, father."

"Thank you, I can manage." He carried the whisky and soda back to his chair. He sipped, brooding, for a while, then took up his pipe again. "Who the devil do they think started this war? The impala? The wildebeeste? And if they didn't, why the hell should they be made to suffer? Churchmen! Bloody people!"

"What about the King of Sweden? Mr. Mackenzie was very impressed."

"He's been taking the stamps again."

"I said he could."

"I see."

"What did the King say?"

He picked up the letter. "His Majesty acknowledges . . . etc . . . etc . . . most interested . . . etc . . . etc . . . however, feels that with the present world crisis the time is not ripe . . . etc . . . etc . . ." He dropped the letter on the pile. "Just the same as the Swiss. Minding their own business. Teddy Roosevelt's the only one who *really* cares but he's not President any longer so there's not much he can do."

"But, father, what can anyone do? Some of the land is in German territory. You've written to the Kaiser, you've written to the King. What more . . . ?"

"The Germans do *not* own the land. It was bought by the Royal Charter Company long before the Hun ever arrived. Good God, after what they did to the farm, d'you think I don't know what they're capable of?"

He began the process once again of getting out of his chair. It was ironic, she thought, that he allowed her to wait on him like a personal servant in everything but this.

The whisky was kept on a circular brass tray in the sitting-room and she could hear the splash of soda. She wondered how long the bottle would last. It was the only one in the house.

As he limped back past her she said, "Supper in fifteen minutes, if that's all right."

"Not for me."

"Later then, I don't mind. It's too hot now, anyway."

"Not for me."

"You should eat something."

He picked up the newspaper that had arrived in the post and began to read. "So much for railways," he said. "The Hun's blown up another section of the main line."

After a while she went into the sitting-room and picked up an old magazine. At nine she went to bed. At intervals during the following two hours she heard him limp from the porch to the sitting-room and back. He went to bed about eleven. She read, under the hot dampness of the mosquito net, until nearly 2 a.m.

# 3

**B**ETWEEN 7.30 p.m. and 8.30 p.m. the two lions came down through the thorny *nyika* towards the railway line.

All that day they had been hunted. There had been the banging of tins and drums, the shouting, even the firing of guns. But no one had seen them, no one had even found their spoor, other than the mass of footprints in the soft soil of the new embankment where they had eaten the *bhisti.*

On one occasion the beaters had come within a hundred yards of where they lay and the noise had caused them to move. They had disappeared silently through the wait-a-bit thorn, keeping to warthog trails. They moved farther from No. 1 camp towards the Escarpment. Both lions were irritated by having to travel in the heat of the day. Late in the afternoon they came upon a cave just where the Escarpment began to swell out of the plain and the ground was broken. It was screened above and below by heavy thorn and was only approachable by a tunnel in the bush that had been made in the recent past by another lion, or perhaps a leopard. There was a litter of old animal and bird bones near the cave mouth.

The young lion found the cave. It was a natural shelter, almost a room, created by huge slabs of red rock that had fallen untidily upon each other in some prehistoric convulsion. He spent some moments at the opening before he went in. He kept up a soft, grating growl that rose slightly as the old lion tried to follow him. The old lion stopped. The young lion began to walk around the cave, urinating. It was some little while before he settled. Only then did his companion come quickly into the cave and lie down.

Now, by the light of a waxing moon, the two lions were dropping down the hillside towards the railway line when they heard in the distance the clack-clack of wheels on the line. They flattened on to their bellies.

Jemadar Singh had been at No. 2 camp investigating a complaint that a tiger had been seen higher up the Escarpment during the afternoon. The Jemadar had lived in Africa for over fifteen years and he knew, or at least he had been told often enough, that there were no tigers in Africa. He imagined the animal to have been a leopard. He was now returning to No. 1 camp. The Superintendent of Works had arrived and he supposed that he and Sahib Kendon would be talking. They might want him at any moment—such was the measure of his importance.

The Jemadar had come out to East Africa from the Punjab as a young man in 1898 with thirty thousand of his fellow-Indians to build the Uganda Railway. He had been a good worker and had prospered. When the line was completed he had, like thousands of others, decided not to return to India, had sent for a wife and made his home in Mombasa.

His father had worked as gatekeeper for an English family, so Jemadar Singh had learnt English. He had also learnt to write. In Mombasa he had made a good living as a professional scribe. He had grown plump, middle-aged and settled. Then came the war and people found it difficult to write to their relatives in India. He was almost destitute when he took a job on the spur line. At first he had worked as a coolie; he, Ragbir Singh! It had been a terrible period of his life. But then Sahib Kendon had arrived. He had wanted someone who could read and write. Someone who could take some of the burden off his shoulders. And so he had made Singh a Jemadar, a headman. He had given him back his dignity, put him back in his proper place in society. He owed all this to Kendon; it was something he would never forget.

With this background, it was not surprising he considered himself a cut above the coolies. He had smiled when they had described the "tiger". If they were to be believed, it had stood six feet high and been as big as a cow; it was a demon, a monster. And yet, as he worked the hand levers of the trolley and sent it along the dark track, he no longer felt like laughing. Perhaps it was because he had seen Karim Ram. While he had been listening to the other coolies he had looked up and seen the big stone-mason standing there, with his great belly and his huge bald head. Singh sensed an utter ruthlessness in the man, a complete disregard for life. Whenever he uncovered serious breaches of the rules, the influence of Karim Ram was somewhere in the background. He knew that Ram was getting supplies of liquor and opium from Mombasa, that he was organizing black whores from Nairobi. A picture filled his mind: the coolie's body swinging from a beam of the water tower, rope cutting into the throat, eyes filled with blood. They had said it was suicide, that the coolie had been unable to bear the heat and the dust and the thirst. But the Jemadar had seen the man's broken fingernails, the mixture of flesh and rope fibres that had accumulated under them. You did not tear frantically at a rope and at your own bare flesh if you *wanted* to die. And then there were the rumours that the coolie had tried to start his own business enterprise, specializing in hemp and opium. It was only a rumour, but it had been enough for the Jemadar to make four out of two and two. He erased Karim Ram from his mind. It was better not to think too much or know too much.

The young lion was to make the kill. A subtle behavioural change had overtaken the two animals since the discovery of the cave. The old lion seemed disposed to hang back.

The trolley came around a slight bend and started on a downgrade. The cutting walls were about five feet high at this point, just level with the Jemadar. As the trolley drew abreast of him, the young lion sprang. He had never made a human kill before and the movement was clumsy. The ground was soft and his hind paws did not grip properly, so half the power of his spring was dissipated. He fell short of the trolley, hitting its side and spinning off on to the track. As he did so, one of his reaching paws knocked off the Jemadar's *puggaree*. The Jemadar began to shout. He forgot to use the levers, instead he stood on the trolley, yelling. The incline was enough to keep the trolley moving and his long hair, released from the turban, streamed out in the wind.

In a few moments he came to his senses. He was alone, the trolley was slowing down. He had no idea what had happened to him. Could it have been the "tiger"? The coolies' fantasies no longer seemed childish.

Just after 6 p.m. that day, a good hour and a half before the Jemadar was attacked, Richard Kendon's servant, Luke, had brought him a message that had come through on the newly completed telegraph line. It stated simply that Mr. Campbell, the Superintendent of Works, would be arriving at Railhead by special train within an hour. Kendon was washing the day's dust from his body when the message came. He had spent most of his day looking for the lion and he was exhausted, for he was no hunter. He had gone after the man-eater because he knew the men expected it. The old Mannlicher with which he occasionally shot small game for the pot was no match for a lion in *his* hands. He knew his limitations. But had he not made the effort the men would have called him a coward—behind his back—and instead of losing part of one day's work he would have lost several in weakened effort. And there was always Karim Ram . . . Kendon felt he was only awaiting an opportunity to make trouble.

He had not seen the Superintendent of Works for some months. Normally it was the Deputy Chief Engineer who paid regular visits to Railhead to check on progress and urge them on to greater effort. The Superintendent had first met Campbell when he came off the ship from Mombasa. War had been declared while he had been at sea and one of the first things he had said was, "Well, Kendon, things have changed. There's nothing in your contract that mentions hostilities. You've every right to stay aboard and we'll pay your passage back home, or wherever you'd like to go."

"As long as I only have to build a railroad and don't have to shoot anyone, I guess it won't be much different from South America."

Campbell was an Aberdonian of medium height, with grizzled grey hair and long-jawed face. It had been shadowed with worry. Now he smiled: "Good man! We'll see you don't have to shoot anyone, and more important, that no one shoots at you." Later, in his office at Kilindini, he had said, "It's been suggested that you accept a temporary commission in the Royal Engineers. How do you feel about that?"

"Do I have to?"

"Not at all."

"Then I'll stay as I am."

Campbell had looked at him thoughtfully. "Perhaps you're right. It's not really your affair, anyway."

At first Kendon had been employed on new track being laid just outside Mombasa. Then he had been sent to the Nairobi shunting yards which the Army wanted to "rationalize". It was only months later that he took over the Kisimi spur.

He went on with his ablutions. The water stank of iodoform. It came from the coolies' bandages. They were all prone to tropical ulcers and grass sores, cuts from thorns and from the razor-like *simis* that were used for clearing the brush. Iodoform was used by the gallon to check the alarming septicaemia rate. He had given strict orders that no one but the Jemadars were to go anywhere near the water, but it was a difficult rule to enforce. By the end of a day of dust and crushing heat the coolies were dehydrated, most men needing to drink between four and six pints to put back what they had lost. If a Jemadar was slow with the ration it was not really possible to blame them for taking the water themselves. Once the smell of iodoform got into the tanks, it stayed.

By the time he had washed and changed he could hear the special coming up the line. In the absolute stillness of the early evening, sounds carried for great distances and the locomotive was more than three miles away when he first heard it. He had given orders for it to be put on the loop so that it would not be in the way of the works train. He walked down to meet it. The sun had gone and the air, although still warm, had lost the fierceness of the afternoon. As he moved, he seemed to stir it so that it touched him with the warmth of new milk. Around him were a hundred cooking fires, the smoke rising lazily, the men lounging near by. It was the time of day when Kendon liked to sit in his folding chair and let the breeze from the southern *pori* dry the sweat on his body; when Luke brought him a whisky and soda; when he took up a book and let the knots in his mind and limbs loosen and relax. He resented having to see Campbell.

As he entered the Superintendent's coach he realized with a sense of shock how primitive his own life had been these past months. The interior was done in green leather against dark mahogany. The coach was split into several large compartments comprising a sitting/dining-room, a bedroom, a bathroom and a small galley. Two Indian servants and a Goanese cook travelled in a second coach. Here in the harsh thorn scrub the coach had a fairytale quality. Campbell was sitting in one of the green leather chairs holding a whisky and soda. "Come in, Kendon," he said. "Come in and sit down." His speech was slightly slurred.

Green blinds had been pulled down over the windows and the light in the coach was the translucent green of the sea.

"The same," Kendon said to one of the servants, nodding towards Campbell's glass.

"Bring the decanter. And the siphon."

With the windows shut, the air in the coach

was nearly boiling. Kendon felt the sweat start out on his body the moment he took the first sip of his drink. Campbell's khaki drill was black with sweat patches.

"Slainte," Campbell said.

"Good luck."

"Aye. Good bloody luck."

When Kendon had met him on the Mombasa waterfront he had estimated Campbell's age at about forty-six or forty-seven; now, as he looked at the grey-white stubble on the cheeks through which tiny runnels of sweat were coursing, he would have said it was nearer sixty: grey hair, grey skin, eyes that were yellow and bloodshot.

"Well, you're still alive," Campbell said. "That's something, I suppose."

"What did you expect?"

"I don't know what to expect any more, except corpses." He waved vaguely at the hooded windows. "It used to be cholera, malaria, dysentery. Now it's maxim guns, six-pounders and dum-dums. And it's only just starting."

He reached for the decanter and poured himself another drink. "Only beginning . . . and already the bush stinks with corpses. The rivers are foul. The waterholes. All down the track you can see the bodies."

"It can't last long," Kendon said. "From all accounts, we're winning."

"We?"

"You see how Anglicized I've become."

"That's what they want you to believe, laddie, but don't you be deceived." As his speech thickened, so his accent broadened. He rambled on about the war, about the British attack on Tanga.

"Our side kept that secret for months. Didn't think we could accept defeat." He drank, staring over the edge of his glass at nothing. "Now the Germans have taken to the bush and we blunder about after them like lost cattle. Perhaps this South African lad, Smuts, will make a difference. At least he's had some experience of fighting in the bush. Perhaps he'll stop these bloody patrols from blowing up my railways."

"I hear they cut the line near Voi last week."

Campbell nodded. "And derailed a troop train. Blew a bloody bridge as it was crossing. Nearly a hundred dead. If they go on like that, they've got us beaten. You're lucky they haven't cut the spur. If there were more waterholes they'd get here. It's something to thank the desert for."

He could not leave the subject of the war. He grew incensed at the British leaders, whom he described as a pack of "base wallahs". It grew dark. The lights came on. They were served with a curry which Campbell hardly touched. The servants raised the blinds. It was black outside and again Kendon was struck by the magical quality of his surroundings. Here he sat in elegance and comfort eating a well-cooked meal while out there, just beyond the black window-panes, was the *nyika* with its complement of horrors. For another moment the dreamlike quality of security held him, then Campbell spoke.

"You're behind!" he said harshly. "You're bloody *weeks* behind schedule!"

Kendon said, "It's in the reports."

"Reports! Listen, those reports are no damn good to me! Steel laid, viaducts built . . . that's the sort of report I want. Records broken. Impossibilities overcome. We don't want bloody reports, man!"

"You can't build this sort of railroad in five minutes! Christ, I've been all over the place and I've never . . ."

"I know where you've worked. Knew all about you before I offered you the job. You don't have to tell *me*. I'm telling *you* there's a bloody war on and the Army's sitting on my neck!"

He threw up an arm, spilling whisky on the carpeted floor. "I've got the new dock works at Mombasa to worry about and new shunting yards at Nairobi *and* the bloody Germans blowing up track, without having to worry about you. A year ago no one in his right mind would have gone to Kisimi. Now it's all I hear: Kisimi this . . . Kisimi that . . . If you ask me it's going to be one of the biggest staging posts this side of Lake Vic. Do you realize what I'm getting at, Kendon?"

"I think so."

"You bloody well know so. They'll have us out. That's what will happen. If we don't keep up, the bloody Army will take over. Twenty years . . . that's how long I've been out here. I've laid track all over bloody Africa and I'm not going to be pushed out by some Englishman in a funny hat with Royal Engineers written on his badges. It's my railway. I built most of it." He paused and said wearily, "Tell me the truth, what's really the matter?"

Kendon realized that what he wanted was something large, dramatic, to take home with him. It was no use giving him prosaic facts any longer, for the Army, who were to judge Kendon through Campbell, knew a million prosaic facts. What would be the use of telling them that they had still not found bedrock for the viaduct piers, or that a flock of guinea-fowl had literally pecked out an embankment from under the newly-keyed steel, or that Karim Ram and his stone-masons were refusing to do piece-work? So he told Campbell about the lion. It was something Campbell, and therefore the Army, could grasp. It had happened before, on the Uganda Railway, in 1898. Lions had stopped work then. It had happened on the Beira-Mashonaland railway and stopped work there. Campbell listened, and seemed almost relieved. He had a story to take back. Then he said: "Maybe you should talk to Storey."

"Storey?"

"The hunter."

"Frederick Seaton Storey?"

"You know him?"

Kendon experienced a slight *frisson*, as though someone had walked on his grave. "Of him," he said. "I thought he was dead."

"Must be, very nearly. But he's the only professional left. Selous, Pretorius, Macklin . . . they're all in the Army. There's no one else. Storey used to be good, so I'm told. You'd better have a word with him if that lion comes back."

"Where is he?"

"He lives on the other side of the scarp. In Kisimi. He's trying to start a national park to protect the wildlife, or something like that. Keeps writing to us about it. We'd have to pay him, of course, but it's worth it. A man-eater can be a bloody nuisance."

They talked for a few minutes more. The drunken energy had drained from Campbell and he slumped in his chair. On the table, the curry had grown cold. Kendon rose to go.

"Seen any Masai?" Campbell asked.

"No. We might be in the middle of India for all the black Africans I've seen."

"You're in the middle of a desert. Anyway, if you get rain you'll see them all right—and their cattle and their flies."

Kendon could not sleep. He told himself he was overtired, but he knew it was not only that. The name Storey had brought it all back. In a way, he was surprised that there

48

should still be an ache. He would have been thirteen . . . no, twelve . . . It was the year he'd had rheumatic fever. The doctor coming and going. A cheery bedside manner. Then low voices in the adjoining room where his mother waited. He caught the word "heart". When he grew older he learnt that rheumatic fever often affected the heart. He had been lucky, there were no permanent after-effects. But that had been in the future, at the time everyone was worried. The house was hushed. His two sisters were allowed to visit him once a day. They entered the room, twisting their fingers, trying to look natural, when really they were bored by his illness and embarrassed by the unnaturalness of their own behaviour.

He had become ill at the end of summer when the wind brought the smell of the high valleys into the house. When he began to get better, Pike's Peak was covered with snow. When he finally got out of bed everything was glistening with spring water.

During all that time his father had been away in Venezuela opening a new mine in the rain forests. He was used to these absences, they made the time together more precious. No one in the family questioned the bond between father and son. It was accepted that this was a special relationship comprising a special kind of love which was not divisible and in which the remainder of the family could not share. They did things together, built things, designed things. He could remember going with his father to Jason's Fork on the other side of the mountain. By then the old mining camp had given up most of its gold and was on the way to becoming a ghost town. "One day there'll be no one working here at all," his father had said. "Except us."

"Us?"

"It's an idea I've had. Using water under high pressure." He went on to develop a theory about gold washing—and more than washing, actually bringing down whole ore-bearing hillsides by undercutting with "water lances", as he called them. Richard had been gripped by the embryonic idea. They had sat in the sunshine above the mining area and discussed ways and means of bringing down the rock from one particularly steep-sided valley. At first neither could see the way past a modification of a rack-railway which would have made the operation too costly. They sat for hours, pretending they owned the mineral rights, enjoying each other's flights of fancy.

And then his father had taken out an envelope
and sketched on it a rail truck with its front
wheels extended downwards on specially
mounted struts so that on an ordinary flat railbed it would have stood up on one end like a
praying mantis, but on a steep line it meant that
a truck could descend and ascend on the horizontal. Its simplicity had taken Richard's
breath away. His father had laughed. "That's
how we'll make our fortune," he'd said.

Richard had just started convalescing when
news came through that his father was dead,
killed in a blasting accident that had brought a
hill down on top of him. The boy had turned
inward. Physically, he had slipped backwards.
"There's got to be a will to live," the doctor
had said to his mother, and the house became
even more subdued. His sisters and his mother
wore black. The blinds were pulled against the
pale sunshine. The only other person to visit
him was Miss Elkins, who taught school. She
asked if he'd like to see any of his friends. He
could hardly remember them. He said so. She
said she'd bring him books. He did not reply.
Two days later she kept her word. He had
glanced at the titles without interest. One was
a collection of sermons, another a series of
Biblical texts. He left them on his table, star-

ing past them, seeing nothing. A few days later, his eyes caught a title which, he always thought later, had been included by mistake. The book was bound in brown leather. In gold lettering on the spine were the words, *A Hunter's Travels in Africa*, by Frederick Seaton Storey.

It is possible that the book kept Kendon alive. At first he had only turned over the pages and looked vaguely at the illustrations. But then, gripped by the confrontation between hunter and hunted, his interest began to grow. He had never read much before, now hour after hour, day after day, he wolfishly devoured the text. He began to form a picture of Africa and its inhabitants. He began to learn about the habits of elephants and lions, giraffes and rhinos. But the part of the book he recalled most vividly was the great fever trek that Storey and his young German companion Kruger had made from Barotseland to Matabeleland. They had been nearly seven hundred miles from the nearest white missionary and both men had been weak with malaria. It had been an epic journey, made more dramatic for Kendon by their ages. Storey would have been in early middle age then, Kruger twenty years younger. It would have been strange if the boy, given the time at which he read the book, had not seen a father-son relationship. And when Storey had to leave the desperately sick Kruger and struggle on alone for help, it was his own father moving out of camp, himself lying bravely in the blankets.

When he had finished the long book he had immediately begun again at page one. By the time he had finished it for the second time he was mending slowly. Since then, although he had not read it again, he had always carried the book with him, a kind of talisman. He had it now, buried under a pile of untidy clothing in his tin trunk.

It was well after midnight before he finally fell into a heavy sleep. At one o'clock in the morning the old lion killed an Indian watchman on the southern edge of No. 2 camp. No one heard his screams and he was eaten by both lions within twenty yards of where he had been sitting.

# 4

THE late afternoon heat in Kisimi reminded Kendon of the moist, woollen climate of the Mississippi at Natchez. There was a low grey overcast which drew the colour out of the roads and buildings and left everything in shades of sepia, the trees black by comparison. Cat's paws of wind skittered across the still, steely lake. He entered the post office. A young woman was collecting mail at the counter. He leant against the corrugated-iron wall and waited. His legs felt weak and his ears buzzed with exhaustion. The voices of the woman and the postmaster came to him as a far-off mumble. After a few moments she left and he went to the counter. "I'm looking for a Mr. Storey," he said. "A Mr. Frederick Storey."

The postmaster frowned, pushing his spectacles up on to his forehead. "I don't know any *Mister* Storey. Colonel Storey, yes . . ."

"The big-game hunter. I was told he lived in Kisimi."

"He's been a colonel for years. Fought in

Matabeleland. Oh, yes, a military man, all right."

"I don't know him."

"No," Mr. Mackenzie said. "And you don't know his daughter, either."

"Daughter?"

"Standing not three yards from you. Anyway, the Colonel's . . ."

Kendon did not wait. He saw her crossing the dusty road and began to run, stumbling on the potholed surface. "Miss Storey!" he called. "Miss Storey!" She turned and his first impression was of a girl, but the outline of her figure in the thin cotton dress corrected that. She was dark with a pale skin and her eyes, which were almost black, were bright and sharp. "I was inquiring the way to your home," he said. "I want to see your father. The postmaster said . . ."

"You were leaning against the wall, weren't you?"

"Yes."

"I thought you were asleep."

"I guess I was, or pretty nearly."

"You're a Canadian?"

"American."

They were outside the Britannia Restaurant and he realized he had not eaten since the previous night. He indicated the door. "Would you join me?" She hesitated. He said, "I know we've not been properly introduced. My name is Richard Kendon."

She smiled. "Well, I suppose . . . if you're coming to see my father . . ."

She had a glass of lemonade and watched him eat three Cornish pasties doused in Worcestershire sauce, a plate of bread and quince jam (there was no butter) and two glasses of lemonade. As he rose and paid, she said, "Is it . . . about the park?"

"What?"

"The park. Is that what you want to see father about?"

"No, it's not the park."

They were outside on the dusty pavement. She looked down at her shoes. It was on the tip of his tongue to tell her why he wanted to see Storey, but suddenly he was wary. Instead he said, "If you . . ."

"He's not there now, I've . . ."

"I'll be glad . . ."

". . . some shopping to do. If it wouldn't bore you. It's only one shop."

"I'd be pleased to."

They went through the town. It was as if the food had sharpened his senses. As they turned out of the main street he saw activity all round him. Sandbags were being laid at some corners, trenches were being dug at others. Of the four or five shops that made up the towncentre all but one had corrugated-iron sheets nailed over their windows. On the upper balcony of Winslow's Hotel he saw a sandbagged machine-gun post. Above the hotel flew the Union Jack. Here and there were soldiers, black and white, in worn and often tattered khaki. On the outskirts there were three hospital tents with a Red Cross flag flying over them.

"At first the war seemed to be happening in another country, but it's coming closer," she said. "There's been fighting less than sixty miles away."

She led the way past the tents towards Patel's shop. The tents lay between it and the town and seemed to isolate it still further.

"Good day," she said, as they entered. Patel was standing on a short ladder rearranging a shelf of tinned goods. He turned and looked at her and Kendon was aware of tension.

"It's hot again," she said.

"Very hot. Very hot." Patel made no move to come to the counter.

"Have you got your book, Mr. Patel?"

Still he did not move. The bills were unpaid. The Army had not come.

"I'm afraid it's quite a long list," she said.

She was *too* bright, *too* cheerful, Kendon thought.

Patel continued to stand at the base of the ladder. The smell of burning joss-sticks was strong in the dim shop. Kendon felt rather than saw Margaret Storey move slightly towards him. She seemed to be expressing something by the movement, a need for support. He said gently to the Indian, "Will you write it down?"

Patel picked up the order book, fussing with the piece of carbon paper that lay under the first page. It was as though he was unwillingly capitulating to superior forces.

They waited. In the same gentle voice Kendon said to her, "Will you read your list?"

Her face was white in the dim light. "Sardines . . ." she began slowly. "Two tins." Standing beside her, he could see that there were very few items on the small piece of paper, but once she began she did not stop for nearly five minutes and in that time ordered many more things—including two bottles of whisky—than she had originally intended.

Mr. Patel's face was impassive as he finished writing. He began totting up the prices, sucking in his cheeks as he did mental calculations. Finally he wrote down the figure and then, drawing a ledger towards him, found the page he wanted and wrote the figure a second time. "Sign please," he said, turning the ledger towards her.

She hesitated. He had not asked her to do this before. Kendon saw the figure at the base of the column and frowned in surprise.

"You going to carry all these goods?" Patel asked, putting the ledger away.

"Can he send them?" Kendon asked her.

"If he would."

"All right. All right."

They walked back through the tented area, along the shuttered street and finally, on the other edge of town, they came to a house with mango trees in the garden and a screened-in porch. During this time they did not speak to one another.

The garden was overgrown, the walls of the house peeling. She stopped him at the gate. The tension and the rigidity were still there.

"What do you want him for?" she asked in a low voice. "To kill something?"

"How did you know?"

She laughed bitterly. "All my life there's been someone at the door. Will the *bwana* come quickly? Will the *bwana* bring the gun?"

"Where will I find him?"

"At the Club. But you're wasting your time. He hasn't fired a gun for years."

Like Mr. Patel's shop, the Kisimi Club stood on its own, but unlike the shop the only people allowed into the building, other than the Club servants, were white. The building was of stone and thatch and comprised two rooms, a small bar and a bigger room with canvas-and-cane furniture, a three-quarter size billiard-table, aspidistras, and old copies of *The Field, Country Life,* the *Strand Magazine* and *Blackwood's.* Around the walls were horns: impala, kongoni, buffalo and Grant's gazelle. There was a puff-adder skin in a glass case and a stuffed tiger fish from the Zambezi River in another. Zebra and kudu skins were scattered over the floor. There were only three people in the entire building: the Indian barman, Storey and Harry Goodman.

Kendon had no sooner introduced himself than he realized both men had drunk enough to make small talk unnecessary, enough, in fact, to lower any barrier of good manners. Later, snatches of the early dialogue came back: the Colonel saying coldly: "We don't want your railway. Don't you realize that? Can't you tell when you're not wanted?" And Goodman, red-faced, sweating in the heat of the small bar, playing at being the Colonel's man with heavy solemnity, pretending to an interest in the game park. He spoke of the Colonel's "vision", boasted about the Colonel's hunting feats—"three bloody buff in three shots"—as though some of the glory would rub off.

Kendon had approached the meeting with excitement. Ever since the Superintendent had told him Storey lived in Kisimi, he had been making plans to visit him. But two more coolies had been killed in No. 2 camp and he had spent three nights sitting up over the carcass of a goat. On the third night he had fallen asleep on top of a pile of sleepers and when he awoke the goat had been taken. He realized, feeling sick, how close the lion must have come. He also realized it was a danger, not only to himself, but to the whole camp. The following day he had walked over the

Escarpment and crossed the lake by the native ferry to Kisimi.

And here was the Colonel, an elderly man with a stick, leaning on a bar-top for support; a shrunken body that had once been tough and hard; grey hair, grey moustache. Was this the man who, with the fever in his body, had walked seven hundred miles to get help to his young companion? Was this the man who had written so movingly of his own closeness to death? He was a cold, inward-looking man, Kendon thought. The only single thing in his favour was that the more fulsome Goodman became, the deeper grew the expression of distaste on Storey's face.

He had not meant to discuss his business in front of Goodman, but there was little alternative, for the big policeman showed no sign of leaving.

"Why don't you pot it yourself?" Goodman said, laughing. "It's easy enough. Ask the Colonel!" He glanced at Storey, but there was no answering smile.

"Because I'm no hunter," Kendon said.

"Everyone else in B.E.A. seems to think he's a dead shot," Storey said, an acid edge to his voice. "Johnny, three more . . ."

"This round's mine," Kendon said.

"You're not a member. On the slate, Johnny." The barman looked doubtful, but served them.

They drank in silence for a few moments, then Kendon said, "Alec Campbell suggested I see you."

"Your Works Super? You railway people won't part with a rupee for my park, now you want me to help you. Well, Mr. Kendon, I don't shoot animals any longer."

Unwilling to accept the decision, Kendon stayed on. He began to feel his liquor. After a while he found himself disliking Storey, not so much for his non-cooperation, but for not being the man he had imagined him to be. Goodman, he simply despised.

"We're not asking you to give your time for nothing," he said at last. The moment he said it he knew he had made a mistake, but by that time he was too tired to care.

Storey stared at him without expression, then he said again, "I do not kill animals."

Kendon left. He walked back into town past the Colonel's house. A lamp was lit and he was tempted to knock, but only momentarily. Just before he reached the hotel he noticed a figure on the other side of the deserted street going in the direction from which he had just come. The man, carrying a book under one arm, seemed familiar. When he was in his room he realized it had been Patel.

The following morning as he was finishing his breakfast, Margaret Storey arrived. "Is there somewhere we can talk?" she asked. He thought of his room with the unmade bed and the untidy mosquito net, then recalled that there was a Residents' Lounge at the top of the stairs. It had clearly not been used for a long time. The air was musty and a thin layer of dust covered sagging Morris chairs and the dried grasses that stood in an elephant's foot near the door. The shutters were fastened and bars of sunshine patterned the floor.

She looked older than the day before. The shadows in the room seemed to collect in smudges under her eyes. "My father is coming to see you," she said. "You've asked him to kill a lion."

"Yes. He said he doesn't shoot any more."

"He's changed his mind."

"Why?"

She did not seem to hear. "I don't want him to go," she said.

"Why not let him speak for himself?"

64

"He's killed enough! Suffered enough! Made others suffer even more."

"I've only asked him to shoot one lion," he protested. "It should be simple enough for him."

"He hasn't shot anything for nearly ten years."

"One doesn't lose the knack."

"There's something you should . . ."

"It was the shop-keeper, wasn't it? The Indian."

"He came to the house last night. I told him father wasn't there. He wanted the money we owe him. He had his book. Then father arrived. He'd been drinking."

"I know."

"He told Patel to stand outside the back door and talk. Patel got angry. He said my father was getting drunk on *his* money. It was awful—father swaying in the doorway and Patel shouting."

"Oh, God!"

"I thought father was going to hit Patel. Then Patel started talking about lawyers and lawsuits and father slammed the door on him and bolted it. Patel stood outside and went on shouting for about ten minutes before he went away."

"We'd pay your father well."

"That's what he said. He didn't go to bed last night. He was still sitting up when I went into his room about five. He did a curious thing. He put his arm around me and kissed me and said you'd made him an offer and that everything was going to be all right."

"Well, then . . ."

"Can't you understand? He's an old man!"

"He was the finest hunter in Africa."

" '*Was*', Mr. Kendon."

He was paying his bill when Storey arrived. They went on to the veranda. The sun was cruel to the Colonel and the ravages of the previous night were plain. He had shaved too closely and with too tremulous a hand and had cut himself in several places. He had stopped the bleeding with tiny pieces of lavatory paper and these, dry and rusty, still adhered to his skin.

"That matter we were discussing last evening," he began. "The lion."

Kendon waited. The old man seemed to be gathering his strength.

"You wanted me to kill it for you."

"You told me you don't shoot animals any more."

"Lions can be a bloody nuisance when they become man-eaters."

Seeing the Colonel in daylight had changed Kendon's mind abruptly. His daughter was right. He was no longer the man for the job.

"I guess that's so. But I've changed my mind about . . ."

"About what?"

"I think I'll have a try myself."

"You!"

"Why not?"

"Look, Kendon . . ."

Suddenly Kendon did not want to see the old man's humiliation.

"I really have to go, Colonel."

For a dreadful moment he thought Storey was going to plead. Instead, his expression changed to anger. "You're a bloody fool!" he said, then he turned and limped off up the street.

His mind was still on the lion when he reached the top of the Escarpment. He'd have to ask Campbell to scour Mombasa and Nairobi for a professional hunter. He'd heard that one or two South African Dutch were still free-lancing. Campbell would have to find one.

He looked down on No. 2 camp. The moment he did so, he knew something was wrong. Where he should have seen the small figures of his workmen plate-laying or clearing bush, there was nothing, no movement, no sound. He began to scramble down the slope, slithering and sliding, pulled off balance by his rucksack. No. 2 camp was deserted. He found a hand-trolley and sent it flying down the track.

At No. 1 camp a curious sight met his eyes. The food and water train had recently arrived and four hundred Indians were perched on it like gulls. They sat everywhere, even on the engine. It was difficult to see the train for bodies.

Jemadar Singh ran to meet him.

"How long have they been here?" Kendon asked.

"They coming yesterday, sahib. In the afternoon. Two *mistaris* were killed, sahib."

"And so? What do they say?"

"They saying they not working, sahib. They wanting bloody beggar killed."

There was no time now for Campbell to find a hunter. "All right," he said. "Tell them I have just talked to the greatest *shikari* in Africa. Tell them he is coming personally to kill the lion."

"When, sahib?"

"When? How the hell do I know when? Tomorrow. The next day."

"They not working, sahib."

"All right! All right! Tell them tomorrow. And then tell the telegraph clerk I want him."

He went to his tent to compose the telegram. It would have to go via Nairobi but if he got it away soon it might be re-routed and reach Kisimi the following morning if the war traffic was not too heavy. He sat on his camp bed with a pad on his knees.

Jemadar Singh stood in the tent opening. "They saying when the lion is dead, *then* they working."

"Who? Who is saying this?"

"Karim Ram, sahib."

He felt sweat break out on the backs of his hands. At some point there would have to be a confrontation between Ram and himself, but not now, because Ram had a point: the two dead men were stone-masons.

There was always money. "Tell the men I will give an extra two rupees to all those at work tomorrow," he said.

Ten minutes later he stood outside his tent and watched some of the coolies drifting back to No. 2 camp. Two rupees. He went back into the tent and picked up the pad: how much would he have to offer Storey to replace the pride he had so casually hurt?

# 5

"OVER there!" Storey shouted. "Pull it over there. Then round."

The dead beast jerked and rolled as the coolies pulled on the ropes. Dust covered everyone.

"No, no . . . not that side! Here . . . round the water tower. And then up there. See that tree? Round the tree . . ."

The heat was appalling in the valley between the two camps. It seemed to rise out of the ground, yet press down out of the sky at the same time. A dozen coolies were heaving ropes which had been tied to the carcass of a zebra. Its belly had been partially opened and as they pulled it left bloody marks on the ground. They had pulled it over as wide an area as possible to lay scent; now they were exhausted.

"This way . . . this way . . . all right. Leave it under the tree."

Storey limped up to the carcass through the settling dust. The coolies dropped down in what shade they could find. The zebra, which

Storey's tracker had shot that morning, quivered and was still.

Kendon had been with the plate-laying gang south of No. 2 camp. The work was going badly. He had lost his temper with the Jemadar in charge. He had threatened to dock pay. It was only when he had run out of breath that the Jemadar, more sullen than cowed, had told him that eight men were missing from the gang. For a second, Kendon had feared a walk-out. Since his return from Kisimi three weeks before, half a dozen coolies had deserted. But these were not desertions. The Jemadar said that the other white man, the *shikari*, had come an hour ago and taken the eight men. He had said he needed them.

At first Kendon did not see the Colonel sitting next to the dead zebra. In fact, he did not see the carcass either, so skilfully did it blend with the sun and shade. He only saw his coolies. He was about to shout at them, for his temper these days was uncertain, when he saw Storey.

"Did you order these men away from the gang?"

"Yes."

"What the hell for?"

Storey's hip caused him to sit awkwardly. He had opened the zebra's belly and brought out the entrails. He was red to the elbows. The smell was bad.

"Because I cannot pull a zebra along the ground by myself, Mr. Kendon." It had been his affectation, since arriving at Railhead, to call Kendon "Mister"; Kendon continued to call him Colonel. The formality hid a certain contempt on both sides.

"But I gave you men!"

Storey worked quickly. "Four men are not strong enough to pull a dead zebra. I'm laying scent. Just because we've had a few days' respite, don't think they won't be back."

Until Storey's arrival, Kendon and the Jemadars and the men had spoken of a single lion. It hadn't taken the Colonel more than a few minutes inspecting the ground at the most recent kill before he said, "You've got two buggers here. One's old, with a bad front paw . . . paws, probably. The other's his mate, I should think."

Storey sharpened his soft steel knife on the leather sole of his boot and began to make small incisions in the meat and entrails. In spite of his disgust at the smell of the open paunch and his anger at Storey's assumption of authority, and in spite of the heat and dust, Kendon found himself watching the old man. It had been a tenet of his father's that any work, done well, had its own fascination. It was something Kendon had learnt from him; he could watch a bricklayer or a cabinet-maker for hours, provided he knew what he was doing. Storey knew what he was doing.

The strange thing was that Storey must have had a similar trait for often Kendon would find him watching the men with their keying hammers. Perhaps he might ask Kendon a question, and for the moment their antagonism would disappear as they became interested—the one in hearing, the other in explaining.

It was such a situation now. He watched Storey open up the belly even further, then he shook a small amount of white powder from a tin on to the blade of a knife. "If you can't shoot him . . . well, then you must make a different plan . . ." He was talking to himself.

"Poison?"

"Strychnine." He began inserting small amounts of the poison into the cuts he had made in the intestines and in the flesh around the anus. He worked economically. His hands, Kendon noted, were steady, his skin looked smoother. He had come out to this wilderness looking old and sick, now he seemed ten years younger. Kendon, on the other hand, felt fifty.

It had taken four telegrams and nearly double the first price to persuade the Colonel to come to the camp. Now that he had, he seemed to have left his conscience in Kisimi. He had entered the world of killing again and seemed to be thriving. Perhaps all he needed was an excuse.

He seemed pleased to have an audience. "Just enough to cover the end of the thumbnail," he said, taking more poison on the end of the blade. "Not too little or he won't feel it, not too much or he'll spew it." Each little cut now had its deposit of white powder. "Dirty buggers, lions," he said. "They always eat arse-first."

"If they eat at all."

"That's right, Mr. Kendon, if they eat at all."

As he sat in his canvas bath that evening, with the smell of iodoform rising from the water, Kendon thought again of the implications of that conversation and depression settled on him. The early evening, with its promise of relaxation, of food and drink, was the part of the day he enjoyed most. And on bath day, the one day of each week on which he felt entitled to take the water, he should have been doubly pleased. But since Storey had arrived much of the joy had gone.

As he soaped himself he tried to put into thought exactly how he felt about the Colonel. There was part jealousy, part envy, part pity, part dislike, part admiration, part gratitude: like everything else it could not be over-simplified. But one thing was clear: Colonel Storey knew how to live in the African bush and Kendon did not.

The Colonel hadn't been there five minutes before he had rejected the area of Kendon's personal camp site. He had not actually made any criticism, but it was implied. He had moved farther up the hill, and instead of using a tent had slung a canvas sail between two trees. He had ordered his mosquito net and camp bed to be placed beneath it and had directed that another canvas awning should be fixed to two trees near by to give shade to the bush kitchen. He had a thick thorn *boma* built around his site. In a couple of hours he had been sitting in his comfortable safari chair, smoking a pipe and looking—as his camp did—as though he had always been there. He had brought with him a tracker, a gun-bearer and a cook-boy from Kisimi and each time Kendon passed his camp he was assailed by the smells of curries and stews, of maize cobs roasting on the coals and the deeply evocative scent of grilling meat. Sometimes when there was a breeze—and that was another thing, Storey got more breeze, having built higher on the rise—the smells would be brought down to his camp, where Luke would be opening the inevitable tin.

But these were surface irritations. The real point was that Storey's arrival just over two weeks before had made him realize how little he belonged to Africa. This realization came at an unfortunate time, just when he was beginning to identify more and more closely. The reason for this was, of course, the railway. He was totally involved with it, to the exclusion of almost everything else. It had become a personal fight to push it on, not for the sake of the Colony or the British Army, but for its own sake: the railway had acquired a life of its own, to which he was bound. Satisfaction now depended upon its progress.

It was ironical that this should have happened when things were going worse than ever. They had re-surveyed the course of the last viaduct and changed its position. Immediately they had struck rock for the foundation of the first pier—and then nothing, no rock at all. The gangs east of No. 1 camp were keying less than half a mile of steel a day on what was a comparatively easy stretch. Then, part of a cutting had collapsed, blocking the track to the south for nearly twenty-four hours; and finally the stone-masons had gone on strike for the four days it had taken Storey to reach them from Kisimi. Kendon was confused. Singly he could deal with such problems, but not when they all came together.

Everything had been all right, he told himself, until the lions had arrived. That was a fact, immutable. Therefore everything would be all right when the lions went. That was also immutable.

But the lions had not gone, either of their own will or under Colonel Storey's guns. And that was the fact that now possessed Kendon. The railway, *his* railway, was being sabotaged. Despite his professionalism, Storey had not dealt with the lions. Since he had been in the camp, four coolies had been taken. Although he had sat up each night over either the remains of a coolie or over a tied goat, he had not had a single shot at the man-eaters.

Kendon finished his bath and Luke brought a towel. "What am I eating?" he asked.

"Majisup," Luke said, by which Kendon understood Maggi soup. "And conbif," by which he understood corned beef. It was a meal he had two or three times a week and one to which he did not look forward. Luke brought him his clothes and a whisky and soda. He sipped it, trying to enjoy the moment.

It was a hot, sultry evening with blue-black clouds outlined in gold by the setting sun. The high thorn *boma* which he, like everyone else, had built around his camp on Colonel Storey's orders, made it even hotter. But the *bomas* seemed to be effective against the lions, which was more important than heat or cold. The most recent victims had all been taken outside their camps at night; two coolies had been on their way to Karim Ram's whores, though Kendon would never be able to prove it. He had thought about the women's presence and had decided that on balance they did more good than harm. He could see the evening breeze stirring the tops of the acacia trees but the *boma* walls effectively isolated him from it. In fact, they isolated him from the entire camp. As he sipped at his glass, he listened. It was barely 6 p.m. yet a stillness had settled over the *nyika*. The men had drawn their water and food rations and had already shut themselves in their *bomas* for the night. It was a strange experience to be isolated in this way. He was used to the teeming ant-heap quality of the camp. Now, cut off, he felt the loneliness more acutely.

Storey came through the narrow gateway. Kendon looked up and found himself smiling at the old man—until he remembered why he was here. It was another of Storey's affectations. On his first day in camp he had seen Jemadar Singh make his report and had decided to copy him. Now, standing in front of Kendon, he began in a precise voice and with formal manner to describe the precautions he had taken that day. He described the spring guns he had set and where they were placed. Then, to Kendon's amazement, he went on to describe the scent-laying and the poisoning of the zebra carcass just as if Kendon had not been there. Kendon kept his face impassive. The Colonel's expression did not change. It was a game they played, neither showing emotion to the other.

Suddenly the ridiculousness of the situation became too much for him. He flung up his hand. "Colonel . . . for Christ's sake! I'm just too tired. Sit down."

Storey hesitated.

"Luke," Kendon called. "Bring the Colonel a whisky-soda."

"No, thank you."

"One won't hurt you."

They discussed the weather. They agreed it was very hot. It would be more pleasant when the rains arrived. When would that be? Kendon asked. In a matter of weeks.

They discussed the war and agreed it was a nuisance and wondered how soon it would be over. Not soon enough, Kendon thought. He had a point there, the Colonel said.

The conversation petered out and the silence grew deeper and Kendon began to wonder whether his own company was not preferable. The very act of asking Storey to sit down had been a weakness, a show of emotion. He stared at the top of the Escarpment which he could see over the *boma* walls.

Storey stared down at his drink. Kendon waited for him to go.

Suddenly, Storey said, "The trouble with a man-eater is that he thinks." He tapped the side of his own head. "He gets too damn clever. You'll see, they won't touch that poisoned bait."

"Then why use it?"

"Must try everything."

"They haven't been near us for a week. Perhaps you've scared them off."

"They'll be back. Possibly found some other animal's kill, or something wounded. I'm told the troops use their machine-guns on anything that moves. If the war lasts any length of time there'll be no game left."

Kendon was tempted to mention the game park, but he had done so once before and had been treated to a frosty stare.

"The men are feeling safer," he said.

Storey was looking down at his empty glass. "Bloody things," he muttered.

Kendon gave him another drink. The war and the weather had been forgotten, there was only one subject which brought them together.

"You know, you sound as if you hate them," he said.

"Don't you?"

Kendon thought of the past two weeks. They were symbolized for him in the limping figure of Storey. Wherever his memory searched he could see the old hunter moving from one point to another, shouting, cajoling, giving orders, always busy. And at night going up into a *machan*—a log platform built in a tree—to wait up over a tied goat. On two nights Kendon had sat with him (not that Storey wanted his company) but exhaustion had finally driven him to his bed. Not so Storey. It seemed as though he needed no sleep. There was a remorselessness about him, an implacability. And yet, so far, he had not fired a shot.

"All hunters hate something," Storey said. "Cunninghame hated leopards. Always said they were the most dangerous game in the bush. Pretorius hated wild dogs. Selous crocs." He sipped the whisky. "They're dirty things, lions. They *like* filth. That's what makes them dangerous when they turn on man. One scratch from those claws can kill you." He talked on, of the habits of lions, of hunting them, of trapping them and even once of eating one. He talked as though the subject chafed at him and expression was his only relief.

In a pause, Kendon said, "But there would be lions in a game park."

Abruptly, as though he was suddenly conscious that he had said too much, Storey rose. "Good night," he said.

Kendon did not want him to leave. "Won't you stay and . . ."

Storey shook his head. He looked old and tired again, a different man from the morning. In the early dusk he was grey: grey hair, grey moustache and grey stubble on his cheeks. He had not taken more than a few steps towards the narrow gateway in the *boma*, a gateway that Luke would now close with heavy thorn branches and so isolate Kendon more completely, when the evening silence was shattered by a scream. It came from less than a hundred yards away, a terrible, rending scream.

Storey stood absolutely still. Then he said, "You'd better stay here."

"Don't be a damn fool!"

They went down the slight slope followed by Storey's gun-bearer with the heavy .400 double. It was almost dark. From all over the valley, pinpoints of light, like winking rivers, converged on the same spot. There was a great deal of yelling and someone was banging an empty tin.

Jemadar Singh came to meet them. "Get rid of them!" Kendon shouted. "Get them into their *bomas*!" The Jemadar went to work with his *lathi*, striking at legs and arms. He was joined by three other Jemadars. They cut a path through the crowd. The smell of smoke from the burning torches made breathing difficult. Storey stopped and grabbed his rifle.

"Get those damned coolies away from here!" he shouted to no one in particular. The bodies fell back. A corpse was there, at their feet. Storey lit a powerful lantern and knelt down to inspect it. One of the arms had been torn out at the shoulder and the whole abdomen cavity was ripped to shreds. All signs of clothing had gone and the body was badly lacerated.

"What happened?" Storey said.

Kendon called Jemadar Singh. "They sitting, sahib. Finish eating. They hearing something . . ." He caught a coolie by the shoulder and brought the terrified man into the centre of the torchlight. The dark,

85

sweating bodies with shining, frightened eyes, pressed closer.

"Mmmm pah! Mmmm pah!" the coolie said.

"That is noise, sahib."

"Then what?"

"Then lion rushing at fence and coming right through, sahib. And taking fellow and going back again. But these men, sahib they throwing burning sticks at lion and he dropping fellow." As he told it, Jemadar Singh shivered. He thought of the demon that had tried to kill him on the trolley. Only something supernatural could go through a wall of thorn branches.

"Let's see the *boma*," Storey said.

The place where the lion had entered and through which it had returned with a body in its jaws, was apparent by the clothing that hung on the thorns. It was more a weakness in the structure than a hole. The lion had forced its way in and forced its way out. Kendon found himself thinking of the three little pigs. This was the home of sticks, huge sticks, whole trees, some of them. What could you do against an animal that could huff and puff such a place down?

"No wonder he was so badly cut," he said,

touching a long, curved thorn. "Incredible that anything could have got through in the first place—and then back again, dragging a body!"

"Sahib!"

Jemadar Singh was indicating something stuck between the thick branches of a felled tree. It was the coolie's arm.

"I want the body," Storey said.

Kendon spoke to the Jemadar, who spoke to the dead coolie's tent-mates. Storey went on with his examination of the ground.

"They say he was a Hindu," Kendon said. "They want to burn the body in accordance with their religion."

"I'm not asking them, I'm telling them."

There was a angry murmur from the crowd closest to the body.

"There'll be trouble," Kendon said.

"This is the first time we've had a real chance. The lions have been cheated. They'll come back. If not tonight, then tomorrow night."

"Can't we use a goat?"

"You build your bloody railway and leave me to get on with my job." Storey reached for his rifle again. "Tell them if they're not gone in one minute, I'm going to fire into them," he said to the Jemadar. He began to count. At thirty the Jemadars went to work with their *lathis*. By sixty the pinpoints of light were winking back to their *bomas*.

"Now let's make a plan," he said.

The mangled corpse had been dropped near the railway track. There were no trees near by in which they could build a *machan*.

"We've no cover," Storey said. "Can't do a thing without cover."

"What about a freight car?"

The food train, due out the following day, was standing farther up the track. "We could uncouple a truck and push it down here."

Storey nodded. "It'll have to do."

Kendon called the Jemadar and the four mess-mates of the dead coolie. In fifteen minutes the truck was in position near the body, giving a marksman a perfect platform from which to fire should the lions return to feed on the corpse.

No. 1 camp took a long time to settle but by midnight there was not a light, not a sound. It was a very dark night. The two men sat in the empty goods wagon and waited. They had now been sitting quite still, but alert, for more than four hours and Kendon was stiff and sore. During that time they had not spoken.

The goods wagon had been used for conveying sacks of rice. It was of the closed variety with sliding doors on both sides. Colonel Storey and Kendon sat on either side of the open door which overlooked the corpse about twenty yards away. They had opened the door on the other side a few feet so that what little breeze there was could change the stifling air.

For some time Kendon's eyes had been playing tricks. It was not that he was sleepy—he was too tense for that—but that his sight varied. Sometimes he could make out the coolie's body as a black patch against a dark background. At others it merged and he could not see it. He found that he had to look up at the sky for minutes on end to rest his straining eyes before being able to pick out the body again. He wanted to warn Storey about this phenomenon, that every now and then he would not be on the watch, but sound, however slight, carried on the still night air. His eyes began to water and he looked up at the heavy dark clouds that obscured the stars. His buttocks were numb and his back was sore. He could not help shifting his weight every little while. He was made more conscious of this weakness by the fact that Storey, even with a bad hip, sat quite still. He found himself resenting the old man again. His, Kendon's, business, was building railways, not sitting up all night trying to kill a lion because the expert had so far failed.

It would not be overstating things, he thought, to say that the whole scheme had been a fiasco. He remembered how confident Storey had been the first week. The staking out of goats, the *machans* that were built. The spring-guns that were set. As he watched him about his work Kendon had recognized the man who had meant so much to him. But day after day, night after night had passed and no shot had been fired, no man-eater had died—no man-eater, apparently, had even been seen. Hero reverted to fallible man—old fallible man, who was clearly past it.

Then there were the dogs.

Dogs, Storey had said, were the best bet. You sent in dogs and they bayed the lion and you shot him. The only thing that had stopped him using dogs was that he had none. Usually you borrowed dogs from a native village, but there were no villages in the desert. So what about Nairobi? They must have dogs there, Storey had said. Kendon had telegraphed to Campbell and two days later a special livestock wagon was attached to the materiel train. When they opened the sliding doors they found fifteen mongrels in individual wire cages. Whether the dogs were naturally bad-tempered or whether it was the hot, thirsty journey from Nairobi, Kendon never knew, but when they were released the dogs fell upon each other. He and Storey and the Jemadars had beaten a roiling mass of fur with their *lathis*, but nothing had stopped them. In less than half an hour six dogs lay dead and the others were streaking for the distant horizon where they no doubt died, for none ever came back to the camp.

Kendon abruptly pulled himself together. He had been staring into the sky for a long time. He looked back at the corpse. He could see it clearly for a moment, then it began to fade into the dark surroundings. Something caught the edge of his vision. Near the corpse was a second dark shape. Or was it his imagination? He looked away, then back. There was no doubt that something was crouching close to the ground. He touched Colonel Storey on the knee and pointed. Storey had the gun to his shoulder. Kendon was aware that his heart beat had accelerated and that his body was trembling. He wanted

Storey to shoot. Why wasn't he firing? Kendon raised the rifle. He could see neither the front sight nor the dark mass he thought was the lion. He looked away and blinked. As he drew the stock into his cheek he suddenly smelt a strange smell, foetid, decayed. Without thinking, he acted. He swung round and fired. The roar of the heavy rifle in the confined space was devastating. The muzzle flash lit up the truck for an instant and he saw, at the open door behind him, the head and front paws of a second lion. It was standing on its back legs, staring at them. Then it was gone.

"Don't move!" Storey said. "He may still be there."

The tremble in Kendon's limbs had turned into an uncontrollable shaking.

In the first light of dawn they climbed out of the goods wagon. There was spoor everywhere. But they found no blood. Kendon was not surprised. His aim had hardly been of the steadiest.

"Sorry about that," Storey muttered. "Bloody inexcusable."

When Kendon went to lie down for a few hours he was still shaking. His fright had a focus now: Why hadn't Storey fired at the first lion? Had he known the other was circling the train? If so, why the hell had he left it to Kendon?

In contrast to the lions, they had put up a poor performance. The lions had been *thinking*. There was no other word for it. For his own sake he tried to erase the picture from his mind. But he could not. There had been—on however primitive a level—a sense of organization; a plan. It was the hunters who had been hunted.

In his own camp Storey had not gone to bed. Instead he had opened a bottle of whisky—he had promised himself it was only for an emergency—and poured himself a drink. His hands shook so much the liquor almost spilled. After three strong drinks the trembling lessened. He sat in his chair trying to recall the circumstances exactly: he had smelled the lion, he had got the gun to his shoulder and then . . . there was a blank. His next memory was of Kendon's gun going off. Why hadn't he, Storey, fired? He simply did not know. And because he didn't know, he was frightened.

By the morning the bottle was half finished;

# 6

IT was the young lion which had killed the coolie; he had made the last four kills. He was also the one which had come around to the rear of the goods wagon. The relationship between the two lions, which had begun to change when they discovered the cave, had remained uncertain. The cause was the swiftness with which the young one was maturing. His coat was a rich buff colour and shone and rippled when he moved. He was sleek, wellfed, and his face, framed by his mane, was unscarred and handsome. By comparison his companion was thinner, scarred, his coat striped by thorn slashes, his mane dusty, matted, and in some parts torn away by the *nyika*.

There was now, in the young lion, the beginnings of a brutal confidence.

Some nights after his abortive leap at Jemadar Singh he had killed the two coolies on their way to Karim Ram's whores. It had been surprisingly easy. He had sprung at one as they walked beside the track and had killed him instantly. The other man had remained still and the lion had made no attempt to touch him. He had straddled his kill, growling softly. Then the coolie had started to run and the lion had killed him, too. It was a maxim that Colonel Storey would have been interested to see played out. He had often said, and had heard other hunters say the same thing, that if you were in real trouble with a lion, the best thing was to stand still. In that way, you might have one chance in a hundred of surviving; if you moved, you had none.

The coolie had moved and the lion had killed him. The bodies had been lying some ten yards apart, which made it impossible for the young animal to guard them both. As he began tearing at the loincloth of one, the other lion had padded softly to the second body. In a few minutes, both animals had been feeding.

Like most relationships, the one between the two lions could not be expressed in simple, general terms. There had been a redistribution of leadership, but the old lion retained his menace, still kept the younger one in awe of him. When he moved to the coolie's body, he did so by right, as though a natural condition now existed between the two lions: youth supporting age.

What had given the young lion his new confidence was his first animal kill. When they had first entered the area of the construction camp, the lions had discovered a waterhole. It was about four miles south-east and about a mile from the track itself, hidden in a tangle of low, rocky hills. They had returned to the waterhole and found a small group of wildebeeste. The young lion managed to kill a fully-grown cow. For nearly a week the lions moved with the herd. Then, when it got too far from water, they returned to their cave.

After lying up for a few days the young lion crashed through a thorn *boma* and dragged a coolie back with him. This was the coolie over whose body Kendon and Storey had sat. Now the younger animal was frightened. The noise of Kendon's gun in the goods wagon, the flash; these things were new and terrifying. Both lions retreated to the cave. The young one was restless. After an hour or two, while it was still dark, he moved out through the *nyika* to the waterhole. His companion followed on burning pads. The old lion was often almost blind with the pain in his paws and jaw, but he still walked with that soft, swinging, arrogant stride that Colonel Storey hated.

In a week, it seemed to Kendon, all was changed. First, the lions had vanished again. Then the men had found rock and the piers of the last viaduct were rising each day. The track was fully laid south of No.1 camp and only the Escarpment lay between it and the lake. But instead of feeling elated he thought of the work involved in bringing the track down the far side—the steeper side—and was a prey to depression.

His relationship with Storey did not help. They seemed more than ever strangers. He decided he must get away from camp, if only for twenty-four hours. He wanted a bed with clean sheets, a bath, food not cooked by Luke, and a safe, cool sleep.

He reached Kisimi early one Saturday afternoon. He could hardly recognize it. Everywhere he looked, there were tents, soldiers, guns, horses, mules. The edge of the lake was busy with vultures picking on the carcasses of bullocks. The smell was very bad in the lake heat. The surface of the main street had been severely cut up by hooves and by the solid rubber tyres of Reos and box-Fords which now stood at the sides of the road along with six-pounders and mountain artillery. He picked his way carefully along the street.

Kisimi seethed with soldiers. He was able to identify sepoys, British Tommies and South Africans. Some wandered slowly up and down the street as though looking for something, without knowing what. Others sat or slept on the pavements, a few had kindled fires and were brewing tea.

He began to feel embarrassed. He seemed to be the only person on the crowded street who was not in uniform. He crossed to Winslow's Hotel. The doorway was crowded with officers. He hesitated.

"What do you want?" an officer asked.

"A room."

"Are you an officer?" This struck the group as being hilarious.

"Kick his arse for him," a voice said.

Kendon shook his head.

"The hotel has been requisitioned. These are officers' quarters now."

He walked farther up the street between groups of soldiers, many of whom stared at him in open hostility. He felt angry and confused. It was not his war; why should he care how they reacted? Yet he did care, not only for his own embarrassment but for the misery and shock on the faces around him. His confusion lay in deciding what to do. He passed the Britannia Restaurant. It had a large Red Cross sign in the window and lines of men stood outside waiting for mugs of tea and sandwiches.

A voice said, "Kendon!" It was Goodman. "Haven't you any sense, coming here in mufti? Get off the street, man!"

"What's happened?"

"Christ, you must be the only one who doesn't know! They were mauled by a German flying column less than thirty miles away. Ambushed near Mopani. Now for God's sake, get off the street! They damn near killed a civilian journalist this morning."

Kendon did not get off the street. He went on until he came to the outskirts of town and found himself outside Colonel Storey's house. It was shuttered, the garden worse than he remembered. The mango trees had been stripped and the branches broken. There was no answer to his knock. He walked around the house, disturbing lizards in the

100

rank grass. The place seemed empty. And suddenly, standing in the crushing heat, he felt empty, too: misplaced, bereft. It was an echo of the feeling he'd had as a child when his father had been killed and he would find himself looking out of a window into the Colorado night, seeing his own reflection in the glass looking in.

He circled the house again, but there was no sign of life. He wanted to be away from Africa and Storey and lions and coolies and soldiers and a war which was not his. He wandered back through side streets until he reached the post office. He could see a line of squatting men among the trees near the lake. He'd had dysentery himself when he had first arrived in Africa. Like the shops, the post office was shuttered and barred. He crossed the road again, running the gauntlet of hostile stares, making for Patel's shop. The area on the outskirts had become one huge conglomeration of hospital tents. Everyone was bandaged or waiting to be bandaged. No one bothered to look up as he passed. He went into the Indian's shop but could get no farther than the threshold. It was jammed with soldiers. He saw Mr. Patel and a woman he assumed to be Patel's wife, and four children he assumed to be Patel's children, darting up and down behind the counter and clambering about on the shelves. All the soldiers wanted to buy; all the Patels wanted to sell. The great, good thing that Mr. Patel had dreamt of, had happened at last.

He was walking back through the hospital complex when he saw Margaret. She and another nurse were bending over a camp stretcher, one of a line of beds set up in the shade of the mango trees. As he went towards her he could hear the buzzing of flies and saw them as a faint, dark cloud above the beds. Her face was drawn by exhaustion.

"Miss Storey?"

The second nurse finished tying a tourniquet around a soldier's leg. Margaret stared at him. Then, as though reaching into her memory, she said, "Mr. Kendon?"

"That's right."

"The lion . . ."

"Yes."

He spoke gently. It was obvious that she was on her last legs. Even as she spoke he could see she was trying to clear her mind. At last she said, "Has father shot it?"

"No." There was a look of sudden relief in her eyes.

102

"How long have you been working here?" he asked.

"Will you take it now?" the other nurse said, preparing to leave.

Margaret nodded and took the strain on the tourniquet. She released the tension at regular intervals. All her actions were dream-like.

"How long? I don't know," she said. She was wearing a stained nurse's uniform and suddenly she swayed. He said, "You must sit down."

"God, no! If I sat down now I'd never get up. There should be some tea. That's what keeps us alive. Hold this . . ."

He took the short stick that was wound into the tourniquet. By turning it clockwise he tightened the ligature. The man on the bed was unconscious, his face the colour of tallow. There was a mass of bloodstained bandages on his thigh. God only knew what wound lay beneath them.

"Here," she said.

He took the steaming mug of over-sweet tea. She drank hers greedily. "I'll take it now." He relinquished the tourniquet.

"How long has this been going on?" he said.

"Nursing? A few days."

"No, I mean this . . ." He indicated the hundreds of casualties.

"They started coming in a week ago, but things became really bad the day before yesterday."

"You need sleep."

A voice said, "Everything all right, nurse?"

"Yes, doctor. This is a friend . . ."

The doctor bent towards the wounded man. "He's dead."

Margaret looked sick and Kendon put out an arm to hold her.

"When did you take over from Nurse Robbins?"

She said in a whisper to Kendon, "When you came."

"About twenty minutes ago," he said.

The doctor seemed very young. He wore a moustache and his eyes were sunk deeply into his head. He straightened up. "He's been dead at least an hour." He glanced at Margaret. "She's had no sleep for thirty-six hours. Take her home. Make her sleep."

Kendon took her arm as they went through the maze of guy ropes and tent flaps. She stumbled forward mechanically. Neither spoke.

The inside of the house was dim. The shutters had not been opened for weeks and there was a musty smell, but the air was cool. As they entered the sitting-room he saw a whisky decanter. He poured her a stiff drink.

She shuddered under the liquor's impact and handed him back the empty glass. He gave her another and she drank half at a gulp.

As she brought the glass away from her mouth it fell to the floor. She was shaking. He took her by the arms. She felt damp, chill.

Gradually the shaking died away. He was still holding her and she smiled. "You're a very gentle person."

"For an engineer?"

"No. Just a gentle person. How long do you have?"

"Twenty-four hours."

He would never forget those twenty-four hours. In fact, they stretched nearer thirty-six, and even then they talked of staying on in the house, when both knew they could not. He never understood clearly why it had happened, except that Margaret had wanted it. Once or twice the next day she hinted at her reasoning and he guessed that this was the first time she had seen life go by default.

She was not a person to plan coldly. She was dominated by instinct and her instinct, at this time, was to experience as much as life could offer. She had been surrounded for nearly a week by the dead and the maimed: in the midst of death we are in life.

In thirty-six hours they experienced all that two people could, except the sharing of a child—and for all he knew that, too, might have been achieved.

They were strange hours. When he was in college it had been fashionable to read Huysmans and he had been greatly affected by *A Rebours*. In the dim, shuttered house, isolated from the world outside, where the light of day came through chinks in the broken jalousies in sharp, translucent bars, mote-filled and hot, he experienced again the sensuality of Huysmans' imagination. Kendon was no monk. He was subject to normal desires and this had always been a problem, living his kind of life. For the coolies there were Karim Ram's whores, and sometimes he envied them. He did what many men had done before him: he tried to keep from his mind those thoughts which disturbed him. When he could not, he either drank too much or went out and tried to shoot something.

Now there was both a tenderness and a ferocity between them. They did not leave the house once, did not even open the door. The strange thing was that neither was shy. Having discarded their clothes, they did not replace them. When they were hungry Margaret made simple meals of tinned food and eggs. Between them, they drank nearly a bottle of whisky. Neither became drunk, instead they seemed to float in a roseate cloud in which every sensation was heightened.

More than eighteen hours they spent asleep, though not in a long stretch. He remembered waking once or twice in daylight and once or twice in the soft lamplight of night. Each time she was awake, as though waiting for him.

When they talked, it was of things long past, of lives that were finished. They did not mention the railway, Colonel Storey, the lions, or the young soldier who had died.

But the war, at least, would not remain ignored. On the Sunday night as they lay in each other's arms, slippery with sweat, they could hear in the distance the thud-thud-thud of artillery. It was then he begged her to come back to the camp with him. He said she could organize a hospital tent where the labourers could be treated for minor ailments instead of being sent all the way to Nairobi. Both knew it was a specious argument.

She said, "No, my dear, I can't." It was a simple, flat statement. When he said he would come back every week-end, and mid-week, if he could, she promised nothing.

On the second morning he awoke at five o'clock and she was gone. He lay on the bed for a long time, unwilling to face the fact that it was over. Then he got up, straightened the bed, dressed himself in clothes he seemed to have removed a long time ago, and left the house.

He walked along the main street in the early light. Clumps of soldiers were sleeping against the shuttered shop fronts. He turned towards the hospital tents, then stopped. A line of wagons was passing Patel's shop, piled with wounded. What could he say to her? What could he do? He turned and made for the lake.

# 7

"ASK him if any more of the stone-masons have been killed."

Jemadar Singh, who was translating, said, "He saying what is difference between stone-mason and coolie? Lions taking coolie last night; maybe taking stone-mason tonight."

"Ask him."

"Sahib, he saying lion can eat stone-mason just like . . ."

"I am not asking him that!" Kendon could feel the sweat drenching his body. In front of him Karim Ram, too, was sweating. There was sweat in the stone-dust on his belly and sweat on his bald head. He was a heavy, menacing figure. The short-handled hammer he held in his right hand and the chisel he held in his left seemed less the tools of an artisan than his weapons.

"I asked him a simple question!" Kendon knew this was fatuous but somehow, in front of so many, he found it impossible to stop.

"He hasn't answered it. Have any more stone-masons been taken?"

"Sahib, he not answering . . ." There was apprehension in the Jemadar's tone.

"For Christ's sake!" They had been going on like this for nearly an hour. Karim Ram, supported on either side by phalanxes of stone-masons, seemed to be quite calm. Hardly surprising, Kendon thought, because he had everything to gain.

What irritated Kendon was that everything had been going so well. The lions had disappeared again. The viaducts on the north side of the Escarpment were surveyed, work had already started on clearing the trees; in a matter of months the Escarpment would be beaten. Then only the few miles to the edge of the lake remained and those wouldn't take more than a week or so. The end really was in sight.

Then, last night, another coolie had been taken. The lion had entered through a weak spot in the *boma* and killed him while he slept. His tent-mates had not even woken up.

Kendon let his eyes travel over the obstinate faces of the masons who had, until yesterday, been cutting the stone for the new abutments. If he sent the lot back to Nairobi, where could he recruit more? What made things worse was Karim Ram's blandness. He knew the big Bengali could speak English, and he knew that Karim Ram knew he knew—and yet they were going through this farce.

"Ask him if the masons are the same as the coolies," Kendon said.

"He saying mason and coolie just the same, sahib."

"Well, why is it the masons get forty rupees and the coolies fifteen? Should the masons not get what the coolies get if they are the same?"

It was feeble, and Kendon saw the contempt in Ram's eyes. Jemadar Singh said, "He saying lion not asking 'You a forty-rupee fellow? You a fifteen-rupee fellow?' Eating up everyone. He saying they want dangerous money."

Here it was again: "dangerous money". If it had not been so irritating, it would have been funny.

Suddenly, he gave up. "Tell Karim Ram that if they go back to work now I will be in touch with Mombasa about more pay."

The Jemadar said, "When?"

"Today. Tomorrow. I don't know. But

soon, soon!" Then, angrily: "Doesn't Karim Ram know there's a war on?"

"He saying it not his war, sahib."

"But he lives here! Doesn't he know what will happen if the Germans come?"

"He saying if Germans come he will still be stone-mason. He will still have brown skin. But Germans may pay more."

For the moment Kendon was beaten, as much by the heat, the lions, the necessity to finish the job, as the implacability of Karim Ram. "All right, tell him I'll telegraph to Mombasa today, but only if they go back to work now."

He had started to walk back to camp when he saw Storey standing in the shade of an acacia tree. He nodded and made to pass, but the old man limped in step.

"You made a mistake there," Storey said. "Never argue with them. They're too clever by half. Rotten blighters, really. Not like the blacks; you can talk to *them*. They've got a sense of loyalty."

"They've got a case."

"Give them something extra and you've got to put your hand in again for the coolies."

"Look at this place! Imagine having to

work here. I guess they're not being overpaid, at that."

"No one forced them to come. I'd be careful if I were you. Funny people, coolies. Once they get it into their heads you're a hard task-master it won't take much to make one of them put a knife into you. That's the way they work things out. If the boss is tough, kill him. The next one they send along might be easier."

"You've just told me I'm a fool to accede to their demands, now you're saying . . ."

"I'm just warning you. They're not like the old native. He's got a sense of . . ."

"I know. Loyalty."

"Justice. By that I mean . . ."

"Anything new?" Kendon cut across his words.

"Do you want my report now?"

Kendon shook his head. He did not want to hear about the number of spring-guns set, the number of dead jackals and hyenas around the poisoned baits.

"There is something . . ." Storey began.

"Oh?"

"I'm not sure. It may be important. Cigar"—he mentioned the name of his Wandorobo tracker—"was out trying for a bait early this morning. He saw something."

"Where?"

"About four miles down the track."

"What was it?"

"I'm not sure."

"All right. We'll take the trolley. I'll get a couple of men."

As they went through No. 1 camp, he noticed a group of coolies working on a large, cage-like structure. They were using steel cable and some old wooden sleepers.

"If you trap one in that, it'll be a miracle," he said.

"Perhaps. Perhaps not. One of them was keen enough to come into the goods wagon. If they won't touch dead baits, we'll give them live."

"You'll never get anyone to go in there. Not for a thousand rupees."

They crossed the four miles of flat scrub on the hand-trolley. The air was still, the sky grey and close. Even their movement through the sluggish atmosphere did not make Kendon any cooler. Cigar pointed to a clump of thorn trees and the coolies brought the trolley to a stop. They walked across the hard-baked earth and behind a low bush they saw a body. It was more of a torso than a whole figure, more of a skeleton than a body. It had lost both its arms; one of its legs had been bitten off below the knee. Some shreds of skin still adhered to bone but it was impossible to tell what the original colour had been. Ants moved in and out of the bone structure but the larger scavengers had gone on to better things.

"Why didn't you tell me?" Kendon said.

Storey looked thoughtful. "I wasn't sure exactly what we'd find. I thought it was a body, but that's all."

"Isn't that enough?"

"You're jumpy. Look again: he isn't one of yours."

"Then who is it?"

"Exactly."

"Masai?"

"Look at the width of the skull. Masai have long Nilotic heads."

"But it could be a native?"

"Could be."

"Bwana!" The shout came from Cigar. He had left the stand of trees and had been moving along the base of a small hillock. Storey and Kendon hurried towards him. They found themselves looking down at a second skeleton. There were a great many prints in the sand around it. All Kendon

115

could make out was that it was some sort of animal, a large antelope, perhaps.

"Well, there's one thing damn certain," Storey said. "Whoever is over there in the trees isn't a woman or a native—or a Masai, for that matter."

"Why not?"

"Because whoever it is rode here on this." He kicked one of the leg bones. "It's a horse."

"A horse?" Kendon used the word as though it described something from another planet.

"That's right."

"Could be a British mounted infantryman. He could have got lost."

Storey nodded. "Or a hunter."

"Or a German."

"Yes. Or a German."

"Lost?"

"Perhaps."

"How else?"

"You tell me."

"How long has he been dead?"

"Difficult to say. A week, perhaps."

"Lions?"

"Or thirst."

"Then he *must* have been lost."

# 8

KENDON was taking the first sip of his evening whisky when he heard a train whistle. No train was due. He walked to the far side of the tent. His new camp was on the Escarpment itself and from it he could look down on the plain. Immediately below him was the now combined workers' camp made up of No. 1 and No. 2 camps. It sprawled in and out of the *nyika*, wherever there was a patch of cleared ground. The tents were pitched in small groups and each group was surrounded by high walls of cut thorn bush. Storey's camp was almost level with his own, but farther from the newly-laid track to the top of the Escarpment. It was incredible, but on this arid hillside Storey had discovered, in a stand of wattle trees, a tiny spring, just enough to give him water for his needs. It had taken Kendon several days to overcome his pride, then he had sent his servant, Luke, with a jug. Now he did so every evening and his whisky no longer tasted of iodoform.

He looked out over the scrub, watching the

train that should not have been there, steaming steadily towards the unloading siding. He drained his glass and went down the slope. As he reached the siding the engine came into view through the trees. It was pulling two coaches. Kendon recognized the first as Campbell's personal coach.

It wasn't Campbell who came down the steps into the stifling evening but a middle-aged Captain of the East Lancs. Regiment. Everything about him gleamed, from his highly-polished riding-boots and Sam Browne to his sparkling cap badge. He was short and square with a thick neck and a ruddy face. In his hand he held a braided leather riding-crop which also gave the appearance of having been polished.

"Good evening," Kendon said, going forward with his hand half-raised. "My name's Kendon. I'm in charge here."

The Captain did not even glance at him. He began to make his way smartly to the rear coach. At that moment a white sergeant descended the steps at one end of the second coach while from the other end a dozen black *askaris* jumped to the ground.

"Fall them in, Sergeant."

The sergeant, a young man with fair hair and a pinkish-white skin, whose uniform bore huge black sweat patches, shouted orders and the *askaris* formed up in a double rank. Kendon watched, bemused, as the Captain walked slowly up and down the lines on inspection. It was such an incongruous sight in the midst of the dusty bush that he felt like laughing, but the Captain's face was serious. The *askaris*, who had been travelling in cramped quarters in the rear of the second coach, were glistening with sweat and in a crumpled state. The Captain made no allowance for either the heat or the journey. Followed by the young sergeant, he inspected his troops as if they had been on parade in Mombasa. Every few paces he stopped and made some comment: "Puttees uneven . . ." He touched the offending leg with his riding-crop. "Take his name, Sergeant." ". . . Button missing . . ." The riding-crop touched the *askari*'s chest. "Take his name . . ." His voice was surprising. Instead of the harsh tones one might have associated with the heavy red face, it was light, soft and cold. ". . . These boots are a disgrace, Sergeant."

"Yes, sir."

"Take his name."

"Sir."

When the inspection was over, he saluted

the sergeant, then turned to Kendon, who found himself looking into a pair of very pale eyes before they slid past his face and settled just above his shoulder. "My name is Brent. This is Sergeant Miller." He pointed to the camp which rose on the swelling ground of the Escarpment. "Coolie camp?"

"That's right."

"Your camp?" The riding-crop indicated the tent higher up. Kendon nodded.

"Sergeant!"

"Sir."

"Look . . ." Kendon began.

"Not now!" Brent said. "Sergeant, we shall make camp to the left of Mr. Kendon's camp. Not too close. I want everything up there. Three messes: mine, yours, theirs."

"Sir."

"I don't know what you're supposed to be doing," Kendon said. "But . . ."

"Don't worry about us."

"Don't worry! I don't know who the hell you are or what you want! You simply arrive here and land yourself on me. I've no idea how you're going to be fed or watered. Then you say, don't worry!"

"We have our own water and our own stores. We want nothing from you. I've told

120

you who I am. The reason for our arrival is simple: *you* are here to build a railway, *we* are here to see that you build it at all speed without unnecessary worry. I suggest you carry on as normal."

Kendon controlled himself. "Look, Brent, there's been some mistake . . ."

"No mistake."

"I mean, we don't need you. You're the only 'unnecessary worry' we've had."

"Has it occurred to you, Kendon, that there's a war on?"

"Christ, how many times have I heard that?"

"Perhaps you haven't taken it in, being an American."

"What's that supposed to mean?"

"It means that since you're not involved in this war your attitude is different from those who are."

"To hell with that!"

"I'm afraid I haven't the time to argue. By the way, there's someone else here. A white hunter."

"Yes. Storey."

"I've heard of him." He turned towards his sergeant.

Kendon stared belligerently at his back.

Brent was old for a captain—and his turn-out was too immaculate. Those British officers he had met had struck him as making almost a fetish of casualness and idiosyncratic sloppiness. No one had worn regulation dress, all had been individualists. This one was different.

"Brent," Kendon said softly, and once more the pale eyes touched him, then hovered in the air just above his shoulder. "I suggest you stop your men. I'm going to telegraph to the Superintendent and find out about this."

"I'm afraid that from now on all telegrams will have to be authorized by me. In a war zone telegraph lines are too important to be entrusted to civilians."

The following morning Brent asked to see the camp area. He asked politely and it would have been churlish to refuse. Kendon had spent much of the night thinking things over and he had come to the conclusion that there was little option but co-operation. Whatever had happened wasn't Brent's fault, he was simply carrying out orders.

He showed Brent the camp and they talked about the man-eaters. Then Brent said he wanted to see the quarry. The heat there, reflected from the rocks, was already intense. Brent asked who was in charge and Kendon pointed to Karim Ram. The big mason had stopped work and was watching them. Brent took out a small notebook and consulted. "His name is Karim Ram?" Surprised, Kendon nodded.

"Would you ask your Jemadar to tell him to bring his men around here." Brent stepped up on to a low rock.

"What for?"

"'I want to talk to them."

"If you've something to say, I'll . . ."

"Please don't make things difficult. I have my orders. If you don't call them, I will." It was said softly, but there was a brutality in Brent's face that Kendon did not miss. The Captain seemed to be two people, one needing constant constraint by the other. For the first time, Kendon felt unsure of himself. There was real power in this man's hands. What he said was backed up all the way along the line by people with increasing power; and finally by guns and ships. Kendon spoke to Jemadar Singh, who walked over to Karim Ram. The stone-masons gathered before Brent.

He kept them waiting long enough for one

or two to begin fidgeting, then he began to speak, slowly, in English. Jemadar Singh translated.

"I come to you from the King across the water," he began, and Kendon thought: God, he thinks he's talking to a group of primitive African tribesmen! "He is our father and our mother. We are all his children. And when children are naughty, they must be punished." The expression on Ram's face became hostile. "You have been naughty. You said you would not work except for more money." He reached into his pocket and pulled out a piece of paper. "This is the telegram that went from here asking for the money. You say you will not work, but you are making a big mistake." Storey was standing to one side of the quarry mouth, nodding in agreement. "The great King our father . . ." There was an outbreak of subdued laughter which Brent ignored. "The great King our father, has sent me to tell you this and to chastise you if you do not listen." This time there was a mutter of anger. It was clear from their reactions that most of the masons understood English. "There will be no extra money. I want you all to hear that." He paused. "*No more!* You signed a contract to work here and in the contract was the number of rupees. You will get no more rupees. You will continue to carry out your work according to your contract."

There was silence. Then Karim Ram spoke to Jemadar Singh.

"He asking, is that all?"

"That's all."

"Then he saying they not working any more. No one making them work."

"Is that so?" Brent stood on the rock, relaxed.

"For God's sake!" Kendon said. "In five minutes you've ruined the work of weeks! You can't talk to these people like children!"

No one was listening to him. Karim Ram had begun to lead his masons out of the quarry.

Kendon ran towards him. "Ram! Wait!"

At that moment there was a burst of machine-gun fire. In the quarry the noise was enormous. Frightened, Kendon stopped, as did everyone else. He looked up. Sited at strategic points on the rim of the quarry and on the walls he could see the *askaris*, each of whom had a rifle trained down at the crowd. On a ledge fifty feet above the ground and half-hidden by a bush, Sergeant Miller crouched over the machine-gun. The burst of fire had not lasted more than five seconds and had been directed about thirty yards ahead of Karim Ram. The dust kicked up by the bullets hovered in the air. A man began to shout. It was like a trigger. The masons ran back into the quarry. Only Karim Ram stood his ground but he, too, was frightened.

Brent was still on his stone. "The first man who leaves this quarry will be shot!" There was no need for the Jemadar to translate, it was clear that new masters had arrived, clear that they were ten times worse than the old.

"You," Brent said, pointing to Ram. "You're under arrest."

Two *askaris* jumped down into the quarry and flanked the Bengali. "All right," Brent said. "Now march!"

It was over. Kendon felt numb. Storey came towards him. "And a damn good thing too! Only way to treat these beggars," he said.

Kendon said, "He went to you last night, didn't he?"

"Brent? No. Early this morning. Before light."

"And you took him to the quarry so he could place his guns. You knew all along."

"Of course. Didn't you? I assumed you'd

got some sense at last. That fellow knows a thing or two. A bit on the strong side, but those blighters aren't like the old African. No damn loyalty. You'll see, they'll work like blacks now."

It was true. The masons were back at work. The *askaris* had moved into the shade, but their presence lingered. They were the living echoes of the shots.

"No," Brent said. "You cannot see him."

They were standing near the rear coach of the train in which the *askaris* had arrived.

"I guess you don't understand," Kendon said. "He's *my* man. I have every right to see him."

"It is *you* who don't seem to understand, Kendon. In wartime, civilians, especially those belonging to a neutral power, have no authority whatsoever. You *have* no rights."

"Look, I realize you have your orders, but sometimes they can be wrong."

"There's been no mistake, I assure you."

"Every construction camp has someone like Karim Ram. All right, he's a rogue. He's got a finger in a great many pies. But the fact is, the men fear and respect him. The only long-term solution is to get him on our side."

"If you don't mind my saying so, that is mawkish rubbish!"

"I've had enough experience to know . . ."

"Force is the only thing these people understand."

". . . how to deal with situations like this."

"You've seen yourself, the others have been working well all morning."

"Don't you see how illogical you're being? You say you've come to guard the track. But now your men will be tied up all day keeping the masons in the quarry and seeing that they work: you're guarding people who are supposed to be on our side."

"Let me clarify something," Brent said. "I did not say we'd come to guard the track. I said your job was to build the railway, our job was to see this was done without unnecessary delay. This line has a high priority. The Army wants it finished. You don't think we're going to let a few coolies slow us down, do you?"

"Sahib! Sahib!" Jemadar Singh was coming through the long grass on the summit of the Escarpment. After his argument with Brent, Kendon had felt unable to remain in camp and had climbed the Escarpment to become absorbed in the problems of laying track on the far side. He had been working with notebook and pencil, looking up every few seconds to the line of white-painted posts with which the survey team had marked the line of track. In spite of the fact that the team had done an excellent job and that the posts traversed the side of the mountain, always taking the easiest gradient, it was going to be a hell of a job.

"Sahib!"

"What is it?"

"Karim Ram!"

"What's happened to him?"

"He very sick."

"Sick?"

"Very, very sick."

"I'll come."

An *askaris* lance-corporal was guarding the coach. "Captain Brent has asked me to look at the prisoner," Kendon said.

"Sergeant say no one must come in." The corporal was large, black, shiny and soft.

"But the Captain asked me to see him. The *Captain.*" The lie, the white skin: they were weapons. Kendon had lied before, but had never used his race. Now he turned to Singh. "The Jemadar will confirm that."

Jemadar Singh's grey-white beard bristled with indignation. "Sahib telling you truly, boy. Why you being so stupid?"

The *askari* moved to one side, then followed them into the coach. It took Kendon some minutes to accustom his eyes to the dim interior. The heat was brutal. The coach itself was divided into two. The far end, behind a sliding door, was where Kendon assumed Sergeant Miller had travelled. The half in which he was standing, would belong to the *askaris*. He recognized the design. It was a type of coach used by the police as a semi-gaol. Campbell had once shown him one, saying that if he had any real trouble with the coolies the Police Commissioner would bring up a contingent and a prison coach.

In one corner was a barred cage. Inside the cage, chained by one arm and one leg, lay Karim Ram. Kendon moved closer. The stone-mason had been beaten about the shoulders and upper arms. The weals were plain. His eyes were closed and he was breathing harshly. His skin was hot and Kendon knew he was suffering from heat-stroke. He opened all the windows. He'd had a bottle of water with him on the Escarpment and he soaked a handkerchief and began to bathe Ram's face and torso. After a few moments the Bengali opened his eyes. Kendon said, "Here, drink." He took the bottle and drank, then Kendon gave him two salt tablets.

"What happened?" Ram stared blankly at him. "Oh, for God's sake, not now!"

Ram spoke in Punjabi to Jemadar Singh.

"Tell him not to be a damn fool," Kendon said, exasperated. He turned to the *askari*. "What happened?"

The corporal shrugged. "Come on duty now-now. He too cheeky, this fellow."

"So because he's cheeky he gets no water, and Captain Brent . . ." He had been about to say, "beats him". The weals, he was sure, had been made by the riding-crop. "All right. Thank you, Corporal. Jemadar, tell Ram he can keep the water. Tell him I'll get him out of here." If he had expected to see gratitude in Ram's eyes, he was disappointed.

He went out into the burning daylight. It was cool compared with the coach. He walked swiftly to the telegraph office, a small corrugated-iron shack near the siding. There was little point, he knew, in talking to Brent. An *askari* stood on guard and the door was shut. The soldier brought his rifle down. The bayonet was fixed. "I must go in," Kendon said. "Captain Brent has said to me that I must . . ."

"You bring Captain. You go inside." This *askari* was solid, bow-legged and tough. He looked as though he had been constructed from tree roots.

"Wait . . ."

The rifle moved. The bayonet was shiny and sharp. Kendon turned and walked slowly back to his camp. He would have to go to Kisimi and telegraph from there. He decided he would leave before dawn.

When he reached his camp, there was a formal invitation from Brent to dine, and he thought it wise to accept.

Storey was already there when he arrived. Brent was affable and Kendon guessed the lance-corporal had not yet reported his visit to Ram.

The Captain had dressed in his mess jacket and his thick red neck glistened with sweat where it emerged from the constricting collar. The dark uniform seemed to make him look stockier, more square.

About twenty-five yards from the tent Sergeant Miller had made his lone camp and fifty yards beyond that, smoke rose from the *askaris'* cooking fires. Below, the coolies and masons were already behind their *bomas*.

"Is it always as hot as this?" Brent said.

"Rains are late again this year. It'll cool down when they come," Storey said.

Brent helped them to whisky. Kendon saw Storey make a gesture of refusal, then drop his hand back on his lap. Brent sipped at a tumbler of soda water. They talked desultorily about the war. Not even Storey, it seemed, wanted to take the stone-masons as a topic of conversation. Brent was very much the considerate host, easy, relaxed, but Kendon visualized him suddenly in the heat of the coach, standing over Karim Ram, saw the flushed face, the swelling neck. He switched his attention to Storey, who had started a conversation about hunting. Brent was describing a duck-shooting trip in the Nile Delta.

Storey's glass was empty. Brent began to fill it and Storey moved uncomfortably on his damaged hip as though he were going to stop him, but again he subsided. He really was useless, Kendon thought; too old, too lame. And yet he could not bring himself to end Storey's contract. He might not be much, but his effect on the coolies alone was worth the money. He made them feel safer.

They ate a bully-beef stew with onions and potatoes, then a tinned Stilton which Brent kept wrapped in damp cheesecloth. They drank Bordeaux with the meal and again Kendon noticed that Brent took only a token glass. Storey was clearly happier with whisky and made no pretence now at trying to stop Brent from keeping his glass charged. Kendon savoured the wine. It was the first he had tasted for months.

Evening turned into night and the hissing pressure lamps were lit. Thinking of Storey brought Kendon's mind to Margaret. She was never very long from his thoughts. Sometimes he could see her face clearly, mostly it was a blur. How would *she* react if he dismissed her father? He had a sudden urge to talk about her, to ask Storey to explain her to him, but Storey would be almost the last person in the world to understand her.

Brent went into his tent and came back with two gun cases. In the few seconds he was away Storey pushed his wine to the side and poured another whisky. Kendon had not seen him drink like this since the Kisimi Club. Brent opened the cases and drew out two rifles. The stocks gleamed sleekly in the lamplight, there was a smell of gun oil. The sights were protected by wadding. Brent put one to his shoulder.

"Feel it!" he said.

Storey put it up. "It's got a good balance. No doubt about that." There was the slightest furriness at the edges of his speech. "But it's not the rifle for lions."

"Try this one." Storey took the second rifle and passed the first, a .256 Mannlicher-Schonauer with a telescopic sight, to Kendon.

"Yes," he said. "It's not bad. But it's not a lion gun either." He passed it to Kendon. It was a .600 express by Jeffreys, with leaf and Lyman sights. "The first's too light and the second's too powerful. What you want for lion is something slow with a heavy bullet. You've got to smash him, hurt him. . . . You've got to break him down, otherwise he's on you."

Brent took the rifles, almost jealously, and put them in their cases. "Both of them have a high muzzle velocity," Storey was saying. "Hit a lion with a solid out of one of those and it'll go right through him and he can still come at you. Now you take a four hundred. That's a real lion gun. I remember once on the Chobe . . ."

"For God's sake, shut up!" Brent shouted. Storey jerked in his chair and his mouth remained open. "How dare you sit there and tell me my rifles aren't suitable!"

"It happens to be a fact. You want a gun with a slow velocity so the bullet will lodge inside the animal. That way its body takes the shock. Then . . ."

"Stop it! I'm ordering you to say nothing further about guns, do you understand me?" In the bright glow from one of the pressure lamps Kendon could see that Brent's face had become curdled by white blotches. "I will not tolerate it!"

"Look, Brent . . ."

Brent turned. "What?" For a few seconds his eyes did not seem to recognize Kendon, but the interruption caused a hiatus in his anger. He turned back to Storey, once again in control of himself.

"I've hunted in the Near East. I've hunted tigers in India . . ."

"Then you should know better," Storey said doggedly.

It was like a slap in the face. When Brent spoke his voice was thick. "I know all about *you*," he said. "You're a joke, Storey. The hunter who doesn't hunt. How long have you been here—three, four weeks? And not a bloody thing!"

"That's enough!" Kendon said, rising from his chair.

Brent ignored him. "You might have been the great *shikari* thirty years ago, but we don't use Martini Henris any more. You wouldn't know what a real rifle felt like!"

Storey was trying to push himself out of his chair and in his agitation was not making a good job of it.

"Look at you!" Brent said. "You drink like a fish. Now you can't even . . ."

A strange voice said, "Begging your pardon, sir . . ."

Brent was shaking as he glanced at the figure of Sergeant Miller stepping into the penumbra. "What is it?"

"Sir, it's Lance-corporal Wamba."

"What about him?"

"I think he's dead, sir."

"Was it that damned coolie?" Brent said harshly. "I should have shot him."

"It wasn't Ram, sir. More like an animal, sir."

Brent picked up the .600 and a bandolier of ammunition and followed the sergeant. Kendon waited for Storey. The old man seemed to have shrunk as he limped down the hill.

The body lay near the steps at the rear of the coach. This time the only light they had was Storey's torch; there was no crowd of agitated coolies, just themselves and two frightened *askaris*. In the torchlight the lance-corporal looked untouched, still polished and plump as he had been in the afternoon. Then Kendon turned him over and they saw that the side of his head had been ripped away.

"How's the prisoner?" Brent said.

"He's all right, sir. Says he heard the animal jump up on to the coach and take the lance-corporal. Says it must have been one of the man-eaters. Says he shouted, and these two . . ." he pointed at the two *askaris*, "came running from the telegraph hut and that's what frightened the animal away."

"One or two lions?"

"Just mentioned the one, sir."

"All right, Sergeant. We must build a *machan* and sit over the body."

"One moment," Storey said. "You may be in charge of your soldiers, but this is my business."

"I told you . . ."

"Brent!" Kendon walked away a few paces and Brent followed. "If you interfere," he said, very softly, "I'll report you. And if something should go wrong . . ." Brent moved back. There was a sudden wariness in his face. Then he turned to Storey. "Very well, you're in charge." He was able to make it sound as though he was granting a short-term promotion.

"You might have noticed that there isn't a tree near enough to build a *machan* in," Storey said acidly. "We'll use the roof of the coach."

They lay on the roof for hours, but nothing happened.

Towards dawn Brent, yawning, said, "They'll never come now."

"This is the time they came before." the Colonel said.

They waited until the pre-dawn grey lighted the cloudy sky. Storey gathered himself and began the painful climb down. "They probably won't come now," he said.

Brent strode off along the path through the *nyika*. Again Kendon waited for Storey. "You can never tell," the old man said slowly. "Never be sure of anything with lion."

There was a sudden thrashing noise in the thicket ahead. Then a gurgling snarl. Then a shot. Storey hobbled faster. Kendon began to run. They rounded a stand of wait-a-bit together and saw a lion on the far side of the clearing about fifteen yards away. Its jaws held Brent by the shoulder.

Kendon could not fire for fear of hitting Brent. He yelled, gripped the rifle by its barrel and ran at the lion. The animal dropped its victim, and sprang into the bush. It paused in full view for some seconds, broadside on, then it was gone. Storey was standing with his rifle in his hands.

"Why the hell didn't you shoot?" Kendon shouted.

# 9

THERE was no bond of blood between the lions. Their relationship had begun more than a year before when the younger one was only half-grown. He had been learning to hunt with his mother when she had attacked a fully-grown sable bull. As she came at him the bull had swept sideways and upwards with his long curving horns and had pierced her belly and chest. They had died on the ground together, interlocked. The young cub had fed on the antelope, nuzzling his mother every now and then, as though to waken her. The old lion had chased the young one away and had eaten what remained of the sable. He was already in pain, already a man-eater. The young one had followed him and had eaten his scraps like a jackal. Two days later the old lion had killed a Kikuyu woman fetching water from a stream. That was the first time the young animal had tasted human flesh.

Now the roles were reversed. The past days had seen a further deterioration in the old

141

lion. He had followed the other to the waterhole and there they'd had two pieces of luck. The first occurred before they reached it. They had come upon a man riding a horse. The young lion had pulled down the horse and the rider had fallen, hurting his leg. He had stumbled into a stand of acacia trees and there the old lion, which had been lagging some distance behind, had killed him.

The second piece of good fortune had been the discovery of a dying buffalo. He was an elderly bull, a singleton, who had wandered across the semi-desert and had arrived, almost dead, at the waterhole. Had he not been so weak the young lion would not have attempted so formidable a kill. But he killed the old bull with comparative ease. The food lasted them for several more days. And then there had been two empty days in which he killed nothing. Hunger drove the two lions back to the railway line and then the railway camp. But unlike their first arrival it was now the younger one which led, the older one following on burning pads, like a jackal after scraps.

That evening they had come out of the cave at dusk and the young lion had taken the lance-corporal from the back of the coach even before full darkness. The old lion had followed him and would have entered the coach when Ram's shouting brought the two *askaris* from the telegraph hut. The young animal had dropped Corporal Wamba and both lions had gone into the *nyika*. They had lain within fifty yards of the coach all night then, in the dawn, the young one had attacked Brent.

The two animals were starving. They had failed twice. As Brent was carried off, they circled the coach and came to the telegraph hut. The two *askaris* who had saved Ram's life were back on guard. The young animal killed the first before the man knew what was happening. The second screamed, dropped his rifle, and ran round the back of the hut. There was no tree big enough to hold him within forty yards, the roof was too high to reach. He turned towards the corrugated-iron walls of the hut and pressed against it, as a child might to escape notice. There the old lion found him. The *askari* did not hear the lion, but smelt him: the smell of decay, the very breath of the charnel house.

When the stretcher party reached Kisimi it was already well past noon. It had been Kendon's decision to bring Brent over the Escarpment. They could have stayed for the works train and sent him to Nairobi but that would have meant hours of waiting and a whole day in a boiling-hot coach as the train returned across the desert. He'd had to decide which Brent could survive. Storey had agreed that he should be carried to the lakeside and taken over in the small ferry.

"He's not too bad," he had said as they dressed the lacerations on Brent's face, back and shoulders. "Blood poisoning is the thing to watch for." The teeth marks were blue holes, like miniature volcanoes. He was unconscious, his normally florid face waxy in the early light. "It's the filth on their claws and the dirt on their teeth that finishes you."

Sergeant Miller had been confused, uncertain, only too willing to follow Kendon's orders. Once he'd been told what to organize, he had done his job well. He had got together a stretcher party, had issued orders about food and water and then helped to strap Brent on to the stretcher.

"Don't worry. I'll keep things going," Storey had said as Kendon was leaving.

Kendon remembered Ram and told Storey to release him.

There were ten of them, eight *askaris*, Kendon and Miller. The first four took up the stretcher poles and began to climb. The sun was just lipping the eastern horizon.

The hospital area had swallowed up almost all the derelict land between the outskirts of the town and Patel's shop. Wagons and mule carts and a few Reos, clanking and shaking, were coming in from the surrounding bush. Whips cracked, drivers cursed, it was a place of chaos. In the midst of all the movement, the sick were being unloaded. Some were being helped along by friends, others, like Brent, were arriving on stretchers.

Kendon stopped at five tents. At each a doctor or orderly waved them away. At the sixth, he saw Margaret. "Not in here," she shouted, her voice raucous, hoarse. "We're full." Her hair had broken out in wisps from under her nurse's bonnet, her face was haggard and her eyes bloodshot. She turned away to care for a soldier whose head was completely bandaged and whom she was feeding through a glass tube.

"Margaret!"

She turned again, focusing her eyes.

There was no immediate warmth. She greeted him as though he was an acquaintance she had not seen for some time. He told her briefly what had happened. She came out of the tent and pointed to a huge marquee that stood by itself. "That's the officers' ward," she said. "They'll look after him."

"All right. And thank you," he said.

She caught the hurt in his voice. She was about to say something, but instead she shrugged and turned away.

They took Brent to the officers' tent. A surgeon looked at his lacerations. "You say it was a lion?"

"Yes."

"He'll be damned lucky to live, then."

The heat, the smell of blood, iodoform and putrefaction combined to make Kendon feel queasy. He left Miller and the *askaris* in the shade of a mango tree near the tent and wandered into the town. There were hundreds of soldiers in the streets. He remembered, too late, what had happened to him the last time he had walked along in civilian clothes. Now he did not care. He knew he had to find somewhere to sleep, even if it was in the shade of one of the shop fronts.

"Kendon!" He looked round and was surprised to see Campbell hurrying after him, drenched with sweat. "Thank God I've found you!"

They went to Campbell's bedroom at the hotel. The officers had moved out under civilian protest and were now occupying the Kisimi Club. Kendon chose a hard-backed chair in case he fell asleep while Campbell was talking. Campbell stood by the window. Although it was not much past mid-afternoon he was drinking whisky in jerky, spasmodic movements. Since they had met he had not stopped talking, except for the brief interruptions when Kendon put a question.

It was clear that Campbell was in Kisimi to save his job. He had received Storey's telegram about the attack on Brent that morning just as he was about to leave Nairobi for Railhead. Instead, he had managed to get the observer's cockpit in a B.E.2C that was flying to Kisimi with dispatches.

He had obviously been at the centre of some intrigue in Nairobi because he had information which was far beyond the limits of civilian knowledge. Kisimi, he told Kendon, was to become the most important staging post for a hundred miles in any direction. It was already the main hospital area. The point he wanted Kendon to appreciate was that the

High Command was split on whether to continue the railway down the Escarpment or build a road around it. The road would be longer, but if the coolies were pulled off the railway and used as labourers it might be completed sooner. Several roads, tracks really, already existed and the job would be to join them up. Campbell, warming to his theme, began to pace the room. "I've been at them and at them all week," he said. "I've told them over and over that we can get the line down the scarp in a few weeks and then . . . good God, there's no comparison with the amount we could carry and the amount they'd get here by road! And we'd do it in bloody half the time!"

Kendon stared at him. He could imagine the intriguing that had been going on: the journeys between Nairobi and Mombasa; the search for influence: the lobbying. He had been to Campbell's home, a modest enough bungalow where Mrs. Campbell had presided over the tea things as though it had been Balmoral. She was an Edinburgh woman with a heavily refined accent. When Kendon had visited the house the children had been away at school in Durban. "They speak so badly," she had said. "It really hurts me to hear them." Even in the moist heat of the coast she had been rigid in whalebone. "I simply hate to hear English being mangled."

". . . and I'm forty-four," Campbell was saying. "If the Army's allowed to take over the railway, that's me finished."

When Kendon left the hotel it was already dusk. He had not realized how long Campbell had been talking. He walked away from the centre of town towards Storey's house. There was a chink of light through the shutters. He knocked on the side door and Margaret's voice called, "It's open." She was sitting on the darkened veranda. "I wondered if you'd come," she said.

He came on to the veranda with its heavy mosquito screening. She was lit faintly from the lamp in the sitting-room. Her hair was brushed out and she was wearing a long loose house-gown.

All the way up the road he'd had to stop himself from hurrying. Now he found himself unable to go forward and take her in his arms. Instead, he said formally, "Did you want me to?"

"I don't dress up like this for every American engineer." She had meant it to sound light, but there was a tension between them. She held out a hand and rose. "I'm

149

sorry. I could see you were upset at the hospital. But that's one world. I don't expect to see people I . . . like there. This is my other world." She pointed to the whisky bottle and glasses on the table. "See? You've corrupted me."

He felt restraint vanish and he reached forward for her.

"Not here," she said.

They took the whisky into the bedroom. "You're over-dressed," she said.

They lay on the bed sipping the whisky and smoking.

"How long do you have?"

"Just tonight."

"While I was wondering if you'd come I was also wondering if I'd have a drink. I think I'm developing my father's taste for it."

"And did you?"

She smiled. "No."

"Then you're not an alcoholic."

She drank and gave a slight shudder. "One of the doctors drinks a bottle a day," she said. "Another is giving himself morphine. When you work alongside them and see what has to be done, you can't blame them. You see I've started smoking."

"You'd better not let your father catch you," he said, half-seriously.

"My father will have to get used to it. There will be a great many things for him to get used to."

"Do you have to . . . ? I mean, go on . . . ?" He waved his arm to encompass the outside world and the hospital.

"It's sickness that will win or lose this war, not casualties. I suppose ten per cent of all our bed cases are wounds. The rest die of dysentery or malaria or blackwater or enteric." She paused. "Of course I must go on. You go on. They go on."

"I guess it seems different."

"For a woman? My dear, this war's going to change many things, but most of all women."

All night they lay in the comfort of each other's arms. Once, just past midnight, he woke and found her trembling and jerking. It was clear she was dreaming and in a moment or two she came awake, frightened. He lit the lamp.

"What was it?" he said.

"I was dreaming about Jeff."

"Jeff?"

"My brother."

"I didn't know you had a brother."

"He's dead."

He could still feel her trembling. "Can you remember the dream? It helps sometimes if you can talk about it."

She shook her head. In the lamplight her face was flushed and sweaty and her hair matted with damp. "It's gone. But I know there was a lion . . . and father . . ."

They had spoken of her father earlier but only on the superficial terms of social inquiry. Kendon realized he knew very little about the family. "Tell me about your brother," he said.

"It's all a long time ago." She was silent for so long he thought she had gone to sleep. Then she said, "In those days we had a farm on the Rufiji River in German East Africa. My father was away after elephant most of the time. Each time he seemed about to settle down and try to make the farm pay he'd hear of one last great herd on the Chobe or the Luangwa or in South Masai Land . . . anywhere . . . and off he'd go in the wagon and we wouldn't hear of him for months. In the end he'd come back, yellow with fever, half starved. The herd would have turned out to be an ordinary one and instead of making us

152

rich, the money from the ivory would only last six or eight months and then he'd have to go again."

"He doesn't look like a farmer."

"He could do one thing and one thing only, shoot. He did it better than anyone. Before he was thirty his name was even known in America. President Roosevelt asked him to take him on safari. He even invited him to shoot big-horn sheep in the Rockies. Father wrote books, too."

"I've read the *Travels*."

"The last one he wrote was *In Search of Big Game*. He put an appendix to the text giving his figures for game shot in a period of . . . I'm not sure how long, ten or twelve years. He thought people might be interested. Instead there was a violent reaction against him. Some reviewers said he had a blood lust. Don't ask me to quote accurate figures, but he listed hundreds and hundreds of animals he'd killed, buffalo and wildebeeste and rhinos and giraffe, elephant, sable, roan, impala, lechwe, pookoo . . . hundreds. The one figure I do remember was the figure for lions. In that time he had shot four hundred and seventy-eight."

"Good God, that must have been a record!"

"That's what the reviewers said. They said he'd slaughtered more lions than anyone else on earth."

"What did he say?"

"He said most reviewers couldn't tell the difference between a lion and a Bengal tiger."

"How did you feel?"

"I remember being angry with the newspapers. We were all angry. Especially Jeff. Father and Jeff were quite different, yet Jeff loved him very deeply. He was only sixteen, gentle and dreamy, but in his own way as familiar with the bush as father was, for precisely the opposite reasons. Jeff loved all living things. He'd have made a wonderful doctor or zoologist. He hated killing anything. Once or twice father had asked him to go with him on short safaris, but Jeff had refused and mother had taken his side. But after the reviews of the book, Jeff seemed to change. He identified completely with father, took his side without question. I don't know whether he really changed, or whether he thought he'd let father down in the past. Anyway, the next time some natives arrived and asked father to shoot a man-eater, Jeff offered to go with him. Of course, father was delighted."

"I loved to go with my father when I was a kid," Kendon said.

"Father had never really spoken much about what happened, but our gun-boy said there was a moment when Jeff could have killed the lion with an easy shot. Father shouted at him to shoot, but he didn't seem able to. He just stood there and the lion went for him."

"Why didn't the Colonel shoot?"

"His horse took fright and threw him. That's how he hurt his hip. The gun-boy killed the lion with the spare rifle but Jeff died six days later of blood poisoning. You could say that the lion killed my mother, too, because she died soon after that. Father wasn't there when she died. He'd gone out with the wagon into the bush after Jeff's death. When he came back, he was an old man. He sold the farm and we came here. He used some of the money to develop a sand and gravel pit, but no one seemed to need sand after a while, because nothing was being built. Then he bought a share in a cattle ranch on the east side of the lake. Rinderpest wiped out the stock. It was after that he began to talk about a game park."

"He told me he'd need four hundred square miles."

"Yes. The whole thing's impossible. It's his way of trying to assuage his own guilt. He wants to call it the Jeffrey Storey National Park."

"You're being pretty hard on him, aren't you?"

"I've lived with him all my life. I had a chance once to get away and live with my mother's relations in Surrey, but how could I have left him? I'm not hard on him. I *know* him."

After a while, they slept. When he closed his eyes he saw again the scene with the lion and Brent, then the lion standing in the bush, an easy target. His mind filled in a detail he had missed in the tension of the moment. Storey's rifle was in his hands. He had not even put it to his shoulder.

They had gone to bed about eight o'clock and both were awake early.

"Lie still," she said. "I'll get some breakfast." She brought in toast, marmalade and coffee and they sat naked on the rumpled bed and ate hungrily as the grey light of dawn seeped into the corners of the room. She leant on one arm, with her legs bent to one side. Her hair was unpinned and fell about her face, her small breasts were firm, her flanks golden-haired. He looked at her all the time as though trying to burn her image into his mind. She was a different person from the previous afternoon. It was as though she left her real personality here in the shuttered house and put on a disguise when she went to the hospital.

"Do you come back home every night?" he asked.

"Yes. Why?"

"I like to know so I can think of you here."

She smiled. "How sentimental you are."

"More than sentimental."

"Oh?"

"In love."

Her eyes slid past him. "You'll spoil it."

"It's true."

"No, it isn't. Just because we've had these precious times, it doesn't . . ."

"Have they been precious to you, too?"

"Of course. You must know that."

"Then it's only natural . . ."

"Don't . . . please! It's the situation. It

heightens everything. Why can't you accept what we've had?"

She cleared the breakfast things and when she returned to the bedroom she was in her nurse's uniform. She seemed stiff and unnatural. The sun was hardly up when she left him. He lay for some time trying to recapture the moment she had brought in the breakfast, the posture of her slim, naked body on the bed. But the pictures were already blurred.

# 10

"SAME principle as a rat trap," Colonel Storey was saying as he and Kendon walked around the cage. It was finished at last, a massive construction of wooden sleepers, pieces of track and lengths of chain. It looked like a narrow oblong box, one end of which could be opened by lifting a type of portcullis by means of chains and pulleys. This was held in place by a lever made from a piece of rail, which in turn was kept in its place by a wire fastened to one end which passed to a spring concealed in the ground inside the cage.

They were standing in the open entrance. "The goat, or whatever it is, is tethered right at the back," Storey said. "Lion comes in this way to get the goat. Treads on the ground covering the spring, the wire's released and, whoosh, down comes the gate behind him."

"What if he jumps against it?" Kendon said. "Won't he push the gate outwards?"

Storey pointed to two rails firmly embedded in the ground, parallel to each other about a foot apart. "The bottom notches into that groove when it drops. Nothing could push it out. Then we build a huge *boma* around it, with only one path up to the cage. Only way the bugger can get to it. Right up to the front door."

Kendon made his way to where Jemadar Singh was waiting with the trolley. He had been down on the flats checking on how the new embankments were standing up and was now on his way back to camp. He was inclined to think that this latest scheme of Storey's was hardly worth the time and labour spent on it. A few days ago he might have put his thoughts into words and Storey would have reacted and there would have been a row and Kendon might have lost his temper and paid the old man off. But that was not the situation now. He had come back from Kisimi two days before and found the camp working smoothly. Karim Ram was reinstated and the masons were well up with the estimates for the viaduct piers on the northern slopes of the Escarpment. When Storey had greeted him with, "Well, we've not broken down," he had been touched by the word "we", for it included not only the two of them, but the camp as a whole. He found his attitude to the Colonel had changed since he had heard Margaret's story. He was more tolerant and the Colonel, in return, was more relaxed. They were also drawn together by a mutual dislike of Brent.

He had not gone back to see Campbell in Kisimi for several reasons. The taint of intrigue had sickened him, but a more important reason was that he had become so at one with the spur line that talk of roads or the Army taking over were mere irrelevancies. No one was going to take over *his* line.

A noise interrupted his thoughts. He paused and listened. It came again, a slight thud, thud, thud of air pressure against his ear-drums; the distant sound of heavy guns.

He took the hand-trolley up towards the Escarpment, pausing, as he did so, by the quarry. He could hear the crack of the stone-hammers. Sooner or later he would have to face Ram. The Bengali had already asked Singh to arrange a meeting but Kendon had put him off. What could he do? Another telegram might bring more troops. In any case, Campbell would hardly be in the mood now to recommend to the Railway Board that the masons should be given more money.

Later that day he was on the top of the

161

Escarpment. The track bed was already beginning to snake down the northern slope, cutting into the side of the mountain, scarring it for ever. It was a sight that had brought an angry reaction from Storey, and even Kendon, whose first love was always the shining ribbons of steel, could appreciate that once they probed into the heart of a land it could never be the same again.

He heard a shout below where the coolies were working and saw a dozen men chasing an antelope up the hillside. It easily out-distanced them and passed close to him. Then he heard a second commotion and saw another buck come springing past. In the space of a few minutes a dozen or more antelope crossed the skyline to his left. His ears picked up the guns again. This time they sounded nearer. He put his binoculars to his eyes and swept the bush-covered plain to the lake and beyond it to Kisimi itself, but the town was covered by a haze of heat, smoke and dust and he could only make it out as a dark area on the lake shore.

That night he dined with Storey. The invitation had been a formal one, on paper, delivered by Cigar, who waited for a written answer.

Storey produced a bottle of whisky and water from the spring. It was tepid, but after the crushing heat of the day Kendon was grateful for it. He noticed that Storey poured his own with a light hand. They talked about the war. From what he had gathered in Kisimi, Kendon told the old man that von Lettow-Vorbeck was allowing the Allied forces to chase him deep into the wilderness; then he would ambush them, cutting them off from their supplies and, in some cases, annihilating them. The Allies were reeling under attacks of fever and dysentery. Even the South African forces whose leader, General Smuts, was now in overall command, had never experienced such conditions. Once the rains came, things would get worse. The black-cotton soil would become like treacle, everything would bog down.

"Bloody people!" Storey broke in, and Kendon was not sure whether he meant the Germans or people in general. "Nothing's going to be the same as it was. When I first came out to this country it was like . . . it's hard to explain without sounding soft. It was like being at the beginning of the world: everything new and clean. There were no motor cars or lorries, just bullock wagons; no high-powered magazine rifles, only single-shot muzzle-loaders."

"And no railway."

Surprisingly, Storey said, "It's not the railway itself that's bad, it's the people it brings."

This was a point that Kendon himself had made in the Kisimi Club when he had gone to recruit the Colonel. He realized for the first time how much the old man had shifted ground since his humiliation by Brent: now he was identifying with the railway, like an old lion with a fixed domain.

"Won't the railway interfere with your plans for the animal sanctuary?" Kendon said.

"The sanctuary will be miles from here, down on the German border. You don't think I'd be here now if the railway was going to interfere with that, do you?"

"It's a great concept. There are a few in the States."

"Old President Kruger started one in South Africa. He showed the way."

"And there'll be no shooting?"

"Of course not!"

"But don't you sometimes have to? I mean, to protect certain species?"

For a second he thought he had gone too far. The Colonel moved angrily in his chair. Then he said, "That's what you have game-wardens for."

The cook-boy served them a venison stew, followed by a compote. When they had finished, Kendon said, "Where do you think they are?"

He had no need to define it more exactly; the lions were still uppermost in their minds, overshadowing even the war.

"Have you seen the buck moving up from the plains?"

"Yes."

"Lions may be feeding on them."

"I saw a dozen coming up the Escarpment today. Couple of kudu among them."

"Something's happening. It's all those bloody guns. They're what's making them move."

"But where to? There's nothing but desert out there."

"I've been thinking about that. You know where we found the body and the horse? It's possible there's a waterhole in the hills near by."

"I thought you said the man died of thirst."

"I said it was *likely*. But look at it this way:

you know how erratic the lions have been. One night they're here, then gone for a week. It would explain things if there's a waterhole. The rider could have been making for it too."

"But what could he be doing there?"

"That's what I can't make out."

At that moment the guns started again. They seemed nearer. Storey shifted uneasily on his damaged hip. He said, "Did you see Margaret when you were in Kisimi?"

"Yes."

"Is she still nursing?"

"Yes."

"Is she all right?"

"Tired. Like everyone else."

"When she was a little girl she wanted to be a nurse. Then again after her brother died. Wanted to go home to train. I said no."

"Why not?"

"Why not? What's a single young girl going to do by herself in England? Then she wanted to be a governess or children's teacher. Which also meant training in England. I said she'd be much better off staying where she was. Anyway, there's the game park. She'll be needed for that."

"How?"

"How what?"

"You say she'll be needed. How?"

"Who do you think is going to look after the house? No, much better for her here in Africa than in some London slum. In any case, she'd be unhappy. I'm all she's got, you know."

"You may find her changed. The war is changing everyone."

Storey shook his head. "Not Margaret. You don't simply change for no reason, not when you've been brought up correctly."

Kendon's need to talk about her was great, but he knew that if they went on discussing her in this way they would end by having a row, and he did not want Storey to learn of his feelings like that.

All that night the guns rumbled. In the early morning Kendon was woken by the telegraph *babu* with an urgent message that a special train would be arriving at noon.

When he met it, his first impression was that the three coaches contained nothing but generals. When he could make out the uniforms more clearly, he saw that some were colonels, some majors. But there were at least two generals, and Campbell was guiding one of them towards him.

He found himself shaking hands with the

Commander-in-Chief of the Imperial Army in East Africa, Lieut.-General Jan Smuts. He saw a man in the mid-forties, the lower part of his face covered by a short pointed beard and moustache. Above it were piercing eyes which seemed to look right into Kendon. When the General spoke his voice was unexpectedly light. "So you're the man who is going to solve my problem," he said.

"For God's sake, Kendon," Campbell said, "there's got to be an alternative to the viaducts!"

"All right! All right!"

They were in Kendon's tent. It was late afternoon and both men were on edge. Campbell began to move about aimlessly. Kendon said, "I'm sorry I've nothing left to drink. I'll get some whisky from Storey if you like."

"Whisky?" Campbell spoke the word as though it were unfamiliar. He took out his cigarette case. Kendon went to the open flap and stood staring out over the *nyika*. He was still angry with Campbell, but that could wait. At the moment, the Superintendent was right. There simply had to be a way. Yet his mind was no nearer a solution than it had been earlier.

From the train, he and Smuts had walked to the top of the Escarpment. Kendon stood a head taller than the General and his long stringy muscles had been toughened by daily slogs up the hillside, but he was hard put to keep up. The General used a stick as long as a Scottish shepherd's and walked with the light step of a mountain man. Soon his staff officers were drenched with sweat and several had dropped behind. As he felt the supple rhythm of Smut's stride, Kendon remembered that this was how his father had walked; light, spring-heeled. He too had been a mountain man.

They had spent nearly two hours at the top. For most of the time, Smuts scoured the countryside through his field-glasses. Kisimi was still enshrouded by dust but the gunfire seemed to have slackened and during the time they spent on the Escarpment only two shells exploded.

After he had examined every square yard of country, he called over an elderly staff officer whom he introduced as Colonel Robertson of the Royal Engineers, and they began an exhaustive discussion of what still had to be done. Slowly Kendon began to realize that they were talking from basic assumptions and facts that were not correct. Their time scale for everything had been telescoped: the delivery of materiel, the loading and unloading; the levelling, blasting, cutting, laying, keying; the sinking of viaduct piers, the cutting and dressing of the stone; in fact, everything attached to bringing the railway line down the northern, steeper slope of the Escarpment, had been trimmed, squeezed, shortened until the schedules looked more like those for laying steel in the flat heart of an industrial country.

As they talked it became apparent that Colonel Robertson was not satisfied and he queried Campbell two or three times. But Campbell seemed to have made up his mind how to conduct the discussion, overlaying it by explanation, smothering some points, confusing others, until finally Kendon saw the General's face twist irritably. It seemed pointless to go along with the pretence and he intervened abruptly to say that the time scales were optimistic, that even if they struck rock for the foundation of the viaduct piers in the first days of digging they would not be able to lay track at anything like the speed which had been discussed. He added bluntly that if the viaducts were as difficult as those on the southern slope they might run as much as a month or even two months over the estimates.

In the silence that followed Smuts stared at him with undisguised annoyance. Then he turned to Campbell. "I understood you to say these were *his* estimates."

Campbell laughed without humour. "Oh, Kendon's a pessimist."

It was only then Kendon had realized that promises had been made in *his* name, and the last of the sympathy he felt for Campbell vanished. He was about to reply angrily when one of the staff officers hurried up and handed Smuts a telegram.

The General read it, his face remaining impassive. "The time for discussion is over," he said. "You will report to me at eight o'clock this evening, at which time you will have plans for an emergency link between here . . ." he indicated where the new tracks stopped ". . . and there." he pointed to the southern shore of the lake. Then he turned to Robertson and said, "Kisimi is invested. We have lost half a battalion trying to fight our way out."

That had been before three o'clock, it was now nearly seven and during the intervening time Campbell had come up with one unworkable suggestion after another.

As he stood at the entrance to the tent Kendon found himself thinking of the semicircle of guns around Kisimi, the overflowing hospital, the columns of wounded. He could see Margaret's face clearly now in his mind's eye. He wondered where she was: at the hospital, at home, hurt, dead? Behind him, he could hear Campbell fretting and fidgeting. The anger he had felt had drained away. It was too late for that now. But if he was to think clearly he had to have some peace.

"I'll be back in a minute," he said. In the grey dusk he made his way to Storey's tent and borrowed half a bottle of whisky. The old man was hunched near the fire.

"Any news?"

"Not yet."

"They're still firing."

"Yes. Occasionally. At least it means Kisimi hasn't fallen."

"Is there anything you can do? I keep thinking of Margaret. She'll be afraid."

"I know. We're trying. We'll work something out."

As he walked back he felt the weight of new responsibility and at the same time a twinge of self-pity. It wasn't his war, yet he seemed to have been made the fulcrum of so many hopes. "You never know how heavy a load you can carry until you pick it up," his father had said to him more than once. For the first time for many years he actively wished his father with him. There was something about Smuts, perhaps only his walk, that had brought back the memory of his father vividly, especially of that last time. . . . He stopped. He stood quite still for more than five minutes, then he began to run. In the tent he thrust the whisky at Campbell. "Pour one for me," he said as he laid a new sheet of heavy paper on the draughtsman's easel that stood on the far side of his cot.

The idea had come into his head in one great molten lump, now he had to separate it into its parts and test each one to see that it worked individually before reassembling them.

Campbell, infected by the sudden change, stood nervously at his elbow sipping neat whisky. "What's it supposed to be?" he asked.

"A truck. A truck that'll go straight down a steep slope!"

General Smuts held a blackboard pointer in his hand and indicated the large-scale map. "Our information is that there are three mountain batteries probably here, here and here." He tapped positions to the north, north-east and south-west of Kisimi. "Between these are heavy machine-gun emplacements, light field guns, rockets and infantry. The only way in to Kisimi or out of it is by boat. The Germans do not possess any craft on this lake. We believe that the two big motor launches owned by the town have been put out of action by shell fire. That leaves a dozen or so rowing boats. When I tell you that there could be as many as two thousand men trapped in the town you will realize how inadequate our transport resources are. Gentlemen, if we lose Kisimi, we can always retake it; if we lose the men in it we lose the means of taking it, at least for a very long time. I want those men out of there as quickly as possible."

"If we could talk to Colonel Robertson,"

Kendon said. "I think there just may be a way."

"We pull out in an hour," Smuts said.

"The problem will be supplies."

"If you can convince Colonel Robertson and myself, you shall have whatever you need."

Kendon nodded. "I'd like you to look at some rough drawings."

The train did not leave in an hour. It was after midnight before it pulled away from the looming darkness of the Escarpment. During that time Kendon had done most of the talking and most of the thinking and, as he watched the red tail-light wink down the track and finally vanish, he felt almost numb with the effort. From the beginning, Smuts and Robertson seemed bent on attacking every suggestion he made. At first he was surprised, then resentful, then slowly it dawned on him that what they were doing was making him think more clearly, that what they were attacking were possible weak spots. When the idea had come to him it had seemed of crystalline purity. Under their questioning it grew blurred. Then as the hours passed he ground it like a polisher grinds a gem-stone until he had each facet clean and clear.

Basically his idea sprang from that last day with his father when they had explored the old mining town of Jason's Fork. They had sat in the sunshine looking up the valley and his father had talked about mining and using water for undercutting ore-bearing hillsides. There had been one particular slope which would not have been suitable for such treatment and they had discussed ways of getting the ore down and neither had had an idea until his father had suddenly taken an envelope from his pocket and done a quick sketch of a freight car with specially designed wheel struts on the front end. It was that drawing that had sprung into his mind.

He had seen and worked on rack-and-pinion railways, cable railways, funicular railways. He had seen tracks in the Andes where the exposure was heart-stopping and where it seemed impossible that a railway could exist. So it was a synthesis of what he had seen, what he had heard, what he had read about and what he could invent that he was now forced to put into some order. The tension in the carriage was palpable. They all knew that the town's safety, the lives of hundreds of soldiers and civilians hung on what they were discussing. They knew they had to get it right *now*, first time, for there would be no other times since time itself was running out.

The point Kendon clung to was a simple one: if they could not go down the north slope of the Escarpment in the normal way, winding back and forth over viaducts and bridges, traversing left and right, if they couldn't do that because of the time it would take, then they must go straight down; they must somehow take the shortest possible line between the top of the Escarpment and the shore of Lake Kisimi.

He started by placing a new sheet of paper on the easel which held the General's maps. At this end of the carriage, under flickering lamps, the four men, Smuts, Robertson, Campbell and Kendon, seemed to be in a private world. The rest of the carriage was given over to the staff: map cases were being pulled out and put away, telegrams sent and received; the air was heavy with tobacco smoke.

Kendon took a thick, soft lead pencil and drew a profile of the Escarpment's north slope. The pencil line descended gradually at first, levelled off, then plunged down more steeply to the valley floor. The entire height of the Escarpment was about nine hundred feet. The upper, gentler gradient stopped about four hundred feet from the summit, where it levelled off for perhaps fifty yards. The second gradient, the steeper one, was about five hundred feet from top to bottom. The upper gradient sloped at sixteen degrees, the lower at forty-five degrees. From the bottom looking up, they had reminded Kendon of skiing-slopes he had seen in New England, but when he tried to describe them he realized the other men had never seen such a slope, hardly knew what it was.

The first four hundred feet seemed easy enough viewed either from top or bottom and, in fact, the gradient was gentle enough to walk on, but sixteen degrees could not be negotiated by a train.

"That's right enough," Campbell said, nodding. "We wouldn't put a train on a gradient of more than two-and-a-half degrees."

Kendon's idea, therefore, was to create on this first slope a light funicular railway. Two sets of lines would be built from the summit to the level ground four hundred feet below, a brake drum would be placed at the top of the slope, and a steel cable passed around it. The ends of the cable would be secured to goods wagons running on the parallel lines, so that a fully-loaded truck descending on the incline would haul an empty truck up. Put as simply as possible, it was like a pulley with two weights, one heavier than the other: the heavier weight will sink pulling the lighter one up.

Smuts nodded and his fingers fretted at his small beard. "Ja," he said finally, "I can understand that. But will it work?" He turned to Robertson, who had been listening carefully. "There's no reason why not," he said grudgingly. "It's a well-established principle in funicular railways. You'll find them in Switzerland and Austria. I think Kendon's idea is possible, but that's the gentler of the two slopes, you'd never be able to do it with a gradient of forty-five degrees."

The General turned to Kendon. "You've brought a truck half-way down. Now explain how you will get it down the other half."

"Okay, the truck's down around the half-way mark. It's on the level ground. That's where a carrier is waiting to take it down the steep grade."

"A carrier?"

"Another truck, only bigger, big enough to carry our normal freight trucks."

"But if the carrier can negotiate the slope, why not our truck?" Robertson said. "The point is that we *can't* use a simple funicular construction. The slope is too steep."

Kendon nodded. "No, there could only be one track down the steep slope, not two." He paused, trying to find words to explain the core of his idea, then he picked up the pencil again. "Perhaps I can show you more clearly on paper."

He sketched as he explained how a truck bound for Kisimi would come down to the level ground by the funicular railway. It would then be hand-pushed along the level stretch. Waiting for it at the top of the steep slope would be the carrier. This was an over-size flat-top truck. It would have normal rear wheels, but its front wheels would be extended downwards so that they held the truck horizontal and would allow it to descend and ascend horizontally. He finished his rough sketch:

"You push the truck on to the carrier at the top of the incline, and you push it off at the bottom on to the track that's been laid to the lake," he said.

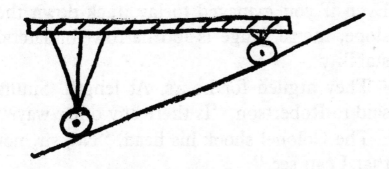

"Wait a minute," Colonel Robertson said. "You've got the truck on *top* of the carrier. You can't push it down on to the line from there."

"We dig a pit at the bottom of the slope. The carrier goes down into it and stops when its platform is level with the ground. Then we can roll the truck off on to the rails."

"Good God!" Robertson said. "It's fantastic! May one ask how you pull this carrier of yours up the slope and how you let it down slowly enough to stop it running away or over-turning?"

"Steam winches at the top of the incline. Heavy steel cable. I think it'll work."

Robertson said, "I'll tell you one thing. You'll never lay track on a slope as steep as that."

"I think I can, if I use eighty-pound rail."

"Another thing: you're laying metre gauge.

181

Even if you managed to lay track down the slope, metre gauge is too narrow for lateral stability . . ."

They argued for hours. At length, Smuts said to Robertson, "Is there any other way?"

The Colonel shook his head. "No, sir, not that I can see."

"So it's Kendon's scheme or nothing?"

"There's the road."

"The road would take weeks, months, and we haven't the motorized transport necessary for an evacuation. At best, Kisimi can only hold out for three weeks or a month. In any case, we couldn't bring up big enough boats on the backs of lorries or ox-wagons."

Robertson shrugged, "I still say it's risky, sir."

The General looked suddenly angry. "All right, Colonel, thank you." He turned to Kendon. "What chance would you say this has?"

"Seventy per cent."

"And you, Campbell?"

"Yes, I'd agree with that. It's *feasible*."

Smuts pulled at his beard, then he said, "How long will it take you?"

Kendon shrugged. He didn't want to be

tied down to hours or days. "It depends on how fast we get the supplies."

"All right. Prepare your lists. They'll have the highest priority."

# 11

THE old lion lay in a patch of thorn scrub and watched the telegraph hut. He had seen the *babu* enter and was waiting for him to emerge.

He was hungry now, after a period of plenty. This had occurred when the two lions were at the waterhole. They had been frightened by a series of shots which had gone on at intervals throughout the day and evening. When thirst drove them down from their hiding-place on a slope of one of the surrounding hills, they saw that a fire was burning some distance from the water and they could hear human voices. Round the waterhole they discovered what the jackals and hyenas had already found—the carcasses of two roan antelope, a warthog and half a dozen guinea fowl.

The following day there was more gunfire and once again at evening when the lions came down to drink there were the newly-dead carcasses of zebra, an ant-eater, several marabou storks, a kudu cow and an impala, and a dozen assorted birds, all lying around the perimeter of the waterhole. The lions fed handsomely.

By the next day the human beings had gone so the lions stayed near the meat. When after a week they had almost finished, the young lion killed a warthog and moved to a different patch of scrub. The old one stayed to eat the last of the zebra meat.

Usually, hyenas made no effort to conceal themselves when lions were on a kill. Now three hyenas watched from dense cover. The old lion seemed to become more and more uneasy. The hyenas moved slowly closer, snarling and whimpering. After a while, the lion abandoned the zebra's remains. The hyenas moved in. It was the first time he had been driven off a kill by hyenas.

He approached the young lion but he raised his head, placed one paw on the warthog's body as though challenging his companion to try to take the meat, and warned him away with a grating snarl. The old lion left the area of the waterhole and made his way through the hills to the railway line. He was almost lame now in his front left leg and when he walked the pad hardly touched the ground. It took him several hours to reach the cave at the bottom of the Escarpment. He lay there all that night and all the following day. The tiny basin of water that replenished itself from a spring was enough to quench his thirst but could do nothing for his hunger. On the third day the griping pains in his empty belly were more severe than those in his mouth and feet and drove him out of the cave in search of food.

The camp had by now moved well up the Escarpment. The lion turned away from the rocky slope and made for the siding where the trains had previously stopped. The telegraph line was being extended along the track but the hut had not yet been transferred. The lion waited for nearly an hour but the telegraph *babu* did not emerge. Driven by hunger he began to stalk the *babu*.

But after the attack on the two *askaris* the hut had been partially rebuilt. In order to keep the *babu* safe, the door was always kept closed; fresh air came through a heavy grille that replaced the window. When the lion found he could not enter the door he became so enraged he attacked the hut itself. It was made of corrugated iron sheets and the lion, goaded on by the screams of the *babu*, pulled and tore at the metal sheets, ripping one

186

almost out of its wooden frame. But the jagged metal cut his paws and legs and he finally stopped. When he returned to the cave he was moving very slowly. He had been without food for nearly four days.

In Kendon's mind the two slopes which made up the cable incline on the Escarpment's north face had become Gradient A (the relatively easy slope at the top) and Gradient B (the steeper, more difficult one that started midway and went down to the plain). Since the night in the railway carriage with General Smuts he had made so many drawings in which he had used this lettering that it had become fixed in his mind. And just as he had never described the Escarpment as "the scarp", he did not now talk about slopes or drops or grades but always of Gradient A and Gradient B. There was respect in his tone, mixed with a little apprehension. The fifty yards of level ground that broke the Escarpment's face, he called the Mid-Level. And it was on the edge of the Mid-Level that he was presently standing.

Had he turned and looked up Gradient A he would have seen first a terrible swathe cut through the trees to the top of the hill, as though made by a giant mower. On this wide, treeless path, two sets of rails had been laid. At the top was the cable drum. Trucks had already ascended and descended: the funicular on Gradient A worked. It was now used for bringing materiel to the Mid-Level for the construction of Gradient B.

Piles of metal and wood lay all around him: winding equipment, 1¼ in. steel cable, the first of the carrier trucks, massive on its stilt wheels, clip drums, 80 lb. rail, steam winches, sleepers. General Smuts had spoken of the "highest priority". Kendon had not appreciated how high that was. He had never met such efficiency in Africa before. It had taken a war to get the country moving and now he only had to telegraph an urgent request for something and it arrived the following day.

In front of him Gradient B dropped away steeply. Once again the trees had been felled and the wide swathe extended to the plain where Robertson was building the four miles of track from the lake shore to the Escarpment. Kendon wondered how he was making out. General Smuts had promised both Robertson and himself protection from possible attack but General von Lettow-Vorbeck had increased sabotage operations on the main line from Nairobi and what men the Commander-in-Chief had to spare were now transferred to guard duty. Robertson's camp was on the southern shore of the lake. If the Germans ever managed to bring boats up he would be vulnerable.

The Escarpment was crowded with labourers and the air was filled with their noise. Kendon had never seen such work. There was a feverish quality about it. Everyone, including himself, was working to the limit of his capacity. What heightened everything was fear: fear of the job itself, but also the fear with which everyone identified, that of the trapped soldiers and civilians. Sooner or later the Germans would break through the Kisimi perimeter; but sooner or later the cable incline would be completed. The almost intolerable tension which tightened Kendon's nerves hour by hour was caused by one question: who would win the race?

He tried not to think what would happen if he lost. He told himself that Margaret was a nurse. No one would harm a nurse; no one fired on hospitals. In fact, there was almost no shelling at all now; everyone said the Germans were conserving ammunition for an all-out attack. But like everything else, it was only rumour.

He watched as a sleeper was manhandled into position near the top of Gradient B. Close by, coolies were sinking holes for the foundations of the steam winches. Things were going almost too well. Gradient A had been completed without a single mishap. Campbell had come to see the tests. He was jubilant, a different man. Kendon wondered if he already saw himself in a big house looking out over the Indian Ocean, a house that came with the Railway Manager's job.

On Gradient B the fish plates lay next to each sleeper; the coolies stood ready with their keying hammers.

"All right!" Kendon shouted. "Let's go!"

Ten coolies stepped off the Mid-Level some distance to his left and began to traverse the slope towards the plate-laying gang. They were carrying a ten-yard length of steel rail. The rail weighed 80 lb. a yard, the entire length weighed 800 lb. They came across the slope very slowly, their splayed toes seeking purchase on each tiny ridge and indentation in the ground. The rail began to sway. The coolies paused. The swaying stopped. The coolies went on. Kendon watched nervously. This was the real test. If he could get the tracks laid he was sure the cable winches would work.

Jemadar Singh joined him. They stood watching as the coolies paused again before taking up the strain.

"It's going to be all right," Kendon said.

"Yes, sahib."

All at once a foot slipped and a man went down. The rail swung round slowly as the others tried to hold it. They were not strong enough. Another man went down. The rail teetered on its end. Then it was rolling and sliding, a shining bar of silver, hurtling down to where a gang of coolies were digging the carrier pit. Kendon shouted. The Jemadar shouted. There were yells of warning from the plate-laying gangs. But the digging continued. The rail was skimming down the slope like a spear on ice. It was on the coolies before they knew it; on them and past in a flash. A second later, its momentum gone, it was lying on the flat ground, a harmless piece of steel. Some yards away were three crumpled bodies.

Kendon came slowly down the Escarpment to his tent. Below him the construction camp was filled with men, an unusual sight for early afternoon. After the disaster all work had stopped. The three coolies struck by the flying column of steel were dead: two instantly, the third an hour later of injuries to his head. When the bodies had been taken back to the camp and everyone had gone, Kendon had tramped over Gradient B by himself, inspecting it more closely, measuring more painstakingly, figuring more carefully than at any time previously and his conclusion remained the same: he was convinced that steel could be laid.

He went into his tent and called to Luke for bath water, then he pulled a bottle of whisky from his military chest. Robertson had said all along that the cable incline on Gradient B could not be built. But Robertson was wrong. As the evening closed in he thought of going to Storey's camp, but they would talk of Margaret.

The next morning he assembled upwards of a hundred coolies on the Mid-Level. The remainder were working on the carrier pit below or felling timber for fuel stacks (the steam winding engines had enormous appetites for fuel), building water towers or unloading the works trains which had now been stepped up to two a day. In contrast

192

with the previous afternoon, the place was alive with workers and yet ... everything was being done lethargically, even though the Jemadars were swearing and in some cases using their *lathis*. Kendon knew that everyone was waiting to see what would happen on Gradient B.

"I want two gangs of ten, to start with," he told Jemadar Singh.

"Sahib, they are saying they not carrying heavy rails on such a mountain."

"Tell them there's no other way."

"They saying there must be other way."

This was not unexpected. Ever since the Army had made the cable incline a priority there had been talk among the men of big money. Karim Ram's "dangerous money" had raised its head once more. Kendon's eyes searched the crowd until he found the big Bengali near the back.

"Tell them I'm not ordering anyone to carry steel on Gradient B," he said, then he played the card that not even Ram could match. "Tell them I want volunteers. Those who carry will be paid an extra ten rupees when the incline is finished. Tell them that. Tell them I need about fifty people." He watched Ram, but the Bengali did not react.

Perhaps he was a spent force. Things had changed for Ram with the building of the cable incline. It meant that since no stone-masons were needed, Ram and his men were now of no more use than anyone else. The moment he realized this, Ram had asked for *more* money, on the grounds that stone-masons should be paid more if they did coolies' work. Kendon had told him he could take his stone-masons and clear out. It was a happy moment. But Karim Ram had not gone, and the reason was obvious: if he chose not to work he would be put on the next train to Nairobi and then what would happen to the income from his string of black whores and his smuggled opium?

Kendon waited. No one came forward. Ten rupees was a big bribe, nearly doubling a coolie's wage. Was it fear of the incline? But there had been deaths ever since the spur line was begun. It *had* to be Ram. He felt a mounting rage. It was time to get rid of him. He should have done it a long time ago.

"Ram!" he shouted, pushing through the crowd. "I want you!"

"Sahib!" The Jemadar put out a hand to restrain him. He knew about the sharpened chisel Ram carried in his waistband. In a crowd like this he could use it once, twice, and no one could swear what had happened. "Sahib!"

"For Christ's sake, let go!"

"Kendon!" a voice cried. "Kendon!"

He stopped. Storey was hobbling down to the Mid-Level. "We've got one!" he cried.

"What?"

"The trap! It worked!"

The entire labour force surrounded the cage. There was an air of suppressed excitement.

"We'd better get that *boma* cleared away," Storey said.

In a matter of minutes, shouting and laughing, the coolies tore away the high thorn walls, disclosing the huge structure of sleepers and steel rails. First there was complete silence, then a concerted gasp, then everyone rushed forward. Kendon and Storey were pulled and jostled until Jemadar Singh cleared a place for them near the cage.

"God!" Kendon said. "He's so big!"

"They always look huge when you see them close up. But he is a big chap."

Coolies were running to higher ground and climbing trees to get a better view. Hundreds more pressed around the cage.

The lion looked at no one. He strode swiftly up and down the twenty-foot long enclosure. There was no sign of a limp and on his face was an expression of utter disdain. In one corner, a small litter of bones and skin were all that remained of the goat that had been used as bait. He stopped his pacing and lay down in the middle of the cage.

"Look at that," Storey said.

"What?"

"His front pads. They're almost gone."

"He's chewing them."

"Poor bloody thing." Kendon looked at him in surprise. "Oh, I know what you're thinking," Storey said with a half-smile. "I haven't changed my opinion of the buggers. But that thing's been in pain for a long time."

"How do you know?"

"I've seen it before. They try to eat porcupines, God knows why, and get a load of quills in their pads and legs. The quills break off leaving the points and it nearly drives them mad. They chew the pads to get rid of the quills. Sometimes they chew until they're walking on raw flesh. Then the feet get infected and the claws come out and they can't kill in the wild so they become man-killers."

The old lion rose and began his pacing once

196

more. The dark mane looked tattered and dusty against the sandy yellow body.

"See those scars . . ." Storey pointed to a series of healed cuts on the shoulders, chest and flanks. "He got those on the thorns of *bomas*. Skin's absolutely ruined."

A stone crashed through the bars hitting the lion on the left side. The animal paused, then took up his pacing. A second stone was thrown, then another and another. "Kill it! Kill it!" a voice screamed.

"Stop them!" Storey shouted.

The coolies pressed closer; their screams were atavistic, filled with vengeance. Scores of voices were shouting, "Kill it! Kill it!" Stones and sticks were beginning to rain down on the cage. Then the lion roared. In the confined space left by the ring of encircling bodies, the sound was terrible. It was so loud, so near, that Kendon felt it vibrate in the cavity of his chest. There was a sudden silence. The men nearest the cage pushed back. The lion turned and for the first time stared at the people, the food, that surrounded him. His stare was at once disdainful and malevolent.

Kendon grasped the moment. "Get back!" he shouted. Storey moved to his side.

Jemadar Singh was there with his *lathi*. The coolies fell back. Then, like children, they turned to Storey and Kendon and began their excited screaming once more. Kendon, terrified, felt himself grabbed by a dozen hands, then all at once he was being hoisted on to shoulders and the men were singing and he could see Storey some distance away and he, too, was being carried aloft.

That night he issued double rations of food and water. He and Storey looked down on the camp. For the first time in weeks it was a mass of lanterns and firelight.

"What are you going to do with the lion?" Kendon asked.

"Send it to Nairobi. I'll telegraph Campbell in the morning. There's been a great deal of interest."

"Wouldn't it be better to put it out of its misery?"

"It would, rather. But Campbell's keen on showing it. Make people think what a devil of a job he's doing. Anyway, it won't harm to leave it where it is for a few days. Just to remind the coolies what we've done."

Storey's psychology was right. The next day Kendon did not have to ask for volunteers. They were waiting for him on the Mid-Level when he arrived.

They kept the lion for nearly a week. Storey sent his tracker out with a rifle and each day he returned with a small antelope. At first the old lion smelt the food and retreated to a part of the cage he seemed to prefer. But after hours during which his roaring could be heard at the top of the Escarpment, he ate heavily.

There was no doubt that he was the centre of attraction in the camp. At almost any time of day groups of coolies could be seen standing next to the huge structure. At first they had continued to throw stones and sticks, but now they simply stared. The lion tended to ignore them as an adult ignores bothersome children.

He had become more than simply a caged man-eater; he was a symbol of the fact that disaster could be overcome. While he was there, the coolies worked with renewed vigour and Kendon was elated. The track began to race down the hillside. It went so quickly that it seemed they would complete Gradient B before Robertson, who had struck boggy ground near the lake, finished the track to the foot of the Escarpment.

But where Kendon was pleased, Jemadar Ragbir Singh was worried, and his anxiety was centred on Karim Ram.

The coolies seemed to have lost their respect for Ram. The Jemadar had not. He knew that Ram had stayed away from work for the past few days feigning dysentery. During that time he had managed to smuggle his string of black women back to Nairobi in an empty works train. Why? Why was he throwing away good money? Was he making plans to leave? If so, there was hardly need for secrecy; Sahib Kendon would be overjoyed to see him go.

The day before, the Jemadar had come down a little-used path and had almost fallen over Ram. The Bengali had been squatting in the bush as though driven there by dysentery. It was only later that Singh realized Ram had been near the locked hut where the blasting powder was kept. Singh had returned to the hut but the padlock was in place and he could not tell whether it had been opened. He went to see the Clerk of Works and approached the question as obliquely as possible. At the end of thirty minutes he had elicited the information that supplies of blasting powder had run out days ago and no more was expected until the following day. He felt better, but only slightly.

Things had changed since the lions had appeared. They seemed to have influenced events in the way that monsters and daemons did in Hindu mythology. Singh remembered the attack on himself and shivered. Yet this time he was not frightened for himself, but for Kendon. He decided to go up the Escarpment by the incoming train; at least on the cable incline he could keep an eye on the sahib.

As he walked past the cage he saw the usual knots of coolies—some were supposed to be sick, others waiting to unload food wagons— gaping at the lion. With a shock, he saw Ram on the far side of the cage. He was staring with great intensity at the lion. Singh watched him for a moment, then went on his way.

"Well, it's all very nice, but will it work?" Robertson said, staring down at Gradient B. "When are you testing?"

"Three or four days," Kendon replied.

"I'll be here for that. And if you're right, I'll eat my hat." It was said in absolute confidence that such an eventuality would not materialize.

"Bloody man," Storey said as they watched him disappear down the slope.

They had spent the whole morning on the Escarpment. Robertson, who had less than a mile left to lay, had said very little, but his attitude was plain. Storey, who had spent the morning with them, seemed to take this as a personal affront. There was no pretence now that he was a hunter. With the trapping of the lion he had fulfilled his part of the contract. He assumed, like everyone else, that the second man-eater had left the area.

But Storey could not have gone if he'd wanted to. There was no way into Kisimi. Kendon was pleased. He had come to depend on the old man's company. There was a nice dichotomy in Storey's attitude to the railway: when only the two of them were together he decried it; but let someone else criticize it and he leapt to Kendon's defence.

Now he said, "I thought you said we'd be testing tomorrow?"

"We will. We'll get the last of the steel laid today. The winches are in and working." Kendon felt a wave of tiredness sweep over him. He rubbed his eyes. All his muscles seemed to ache. "I want a clear run. If Robertson had his way he'd whistle up the entire General Staff to come and watch."

"Bloody man!" Storey repeated.

"He's all right, I guess. I just don't want him breathing down my neck in case something goes wrong."

"Nothing will go wrong," Storey said.

"No. Nothing will go wrong."

But although everything was ready they did not test Gradient B the next day. Kendon knew that something was wrong even before he set out for the Mid-Level. It was a morning for things to go wrong: blue-black clouds overhead and thunder in the hot air. Usually he was at his breakfast when the works train carrying the coolies came slowly past on its way to the top of the Escarpment. But this morning there was no train. He hurried down to the camp. It too was empty. "Sahib! Sahib!" Jemadar Singh, breathless, caught up with him.

"What's up? What's happening?"

"It is the lion, sahib."

"Escaped!"

"No, sahib."

"What, then?"

But Jemadar Singh could not explain, it was beyond explanation. He led Kendon through the press of coolies around the cage. When Kendon saw what was inside he felt ill. Storey was already there, his face white and sweaty, a muscle twitching in his cheek.

The lion was lying on its side in a great pool of blood. The body was a mass of stab wounds and one of the eye sockets was empty. None of the wounds was very deep; it was as though whoever had done this had not wanted the animal to die quickly. As it breathed, bubbles of blood frothed at its mouth.

"How the hell did it happen?" Kendon said.

"Someone with a long-handled spear could have done it."

"Have you seen a spear in the camp?"

"A knife?"

"Couldn't have got close enough. No, it's got to have been something with a long handle."

"But wouldn't someone have heard?"

"I heard him roaring all right. But he's done it every night. Most of the day as well. And no one leaves the *bomas* after dark; none of these brave lads anyway."

"You can't blame them."

"No?" Colonel Storey worked the bolt of his rifle. "Tell them to move." He seemed about to bring the gun to his shoulder when suddenly he passed it to Cigar. "Shoot it," he said. The lion was already near to death and hardly felt the comfort of the bullet. By the time Cigar had fired again, life had fled. The two men entered the narrow cage. Storey bent over the carcass and inspected the front pads. "Difficult to say if it was a porcupine or not." The pads were eaten away, the flesh beneath suppurating. Storey indicated the animal's mouth. One side of it was gone, showing the teeth in a leer. It too had been eaten away; there were maggots in the skin.

"We'd better get him buried before he begins to stink," he said.

The Jemadar issued orders. None of the coolies responded. As the Jemadar called to each man, he turned and lost himself in the crowd. A trickle began to make for the camp. In seconds the whole mob was moving away. Storey, Kendon and Jemadar Singh found themselves alone. It was as though the coolies knew that retribution would come from such an act. There was fear in the air, a menace less tangible but as real as the lion itself.

"I'll get my chaps to do it," Storey said.

"Who the hell could *think* of such a thing, much less do it?" Kendon said bitterly.

"Don't forget, to them he was the enemy," Storey said.

"Even so . . ."

The Jemadar knew who could think of such a thing. He did not even allow the name to penetrate his mind. The sahib had talked of a spear, but what of a sharpened stone-chisel forced into a bamboo shaft? Would not that do just as well?

Kendon turned to the Jemadar. "I want them on the Mid-Level in an hour."

The Jemadar looked at him in astonishment. The sahib clearly did not understand. No one was going to work that day, nor perhaps the next nor the next.

"Just when things were going well! That's what makes me so mad," Kendon said.

It was early evening and they were in Storey's camp, each with a whisky. Storey had already had several and his speech was slightly thickened.

"It's not being able to *do* anything about it," he said at last and Kendon knew he was thinking, not about the railway, but about his

206

inability to do anything about the people of Kisimi. Yet the two things grew out of each other. The railway was the answer. If Kendon had allowed himself to think of Margaret he might have given way to despair. All that day he had struggled to get the men to work. They had looked at him with dark fearful eyes and when he spoke they had turned away.

The bombardment had started an hour earlier and seemed to have gone on longer than usual. Were the Germans getting fresh supplies of ammunition?

Storey had begun to drink after the guns had started and Kendon could not blame him.

At length he said, "I'm putting Ram on the train tomorrow. And all his masons."

"You're sure he did it?"

"Ask yourself. Yesterday he'd lost their respect and everyone was working. Today no one works and everyone is afraid. All that's happened in the interim is that a lion has been mutilated. It was his way of showing he wasn't finished."

"Maybe. But it could also be any friend of one of the dead coolies. How many have been killed by the lions?"

"Twelve."

"Well, if each man had two friends that makes twenty-four with reason to have done it."

"I still think it's Ram."

"You'll have trouble."

"I'll need moral support."

Storey tapped the butt of the rifle leaning against his chair. "I'll give you more than that. Have a drink."

Kendon shook his head.

"Oh, for God's sake, let yourself go for once!"

He drank too much and slept heavily, so heavily that at first he failed to wake up when told to. He was fuddled, dizzy. Then he felt something cold and hard press into his neck. It took him a moment or two to realize it was a revolver.

"Get up!" a voice said evenly.

# 12

HE tried to make sense of what was happening. The lamp had been lit and two men were stooping over his cot. Both had revolvers. They were dressed in South African uniforms which were covered in dust and their cheeks were dark with stubble. In the lamplight he could see their bloodshot eyes.

"Get up!" the first man said again. His voice was heavily accented.

He was a large man with short blond hair and a skin that had been burnt to the texture of leather. Each time he moved, his belt and boots creaked. There was something desert-like about him, as though he had grown in a waterless country: fibrous, sinewy, tough. Why the hell, Kendon thought angrily as he began to dress, would a South African hold a gun at his head?

Then the officer spoke quickly to the other man, a sergeant, and he realized he was listening, not to South African Dutch, but German.

209

The sergeant began to search the tent, rummaging through the trunks. Kendon stopped dressing and watched. "Is he looking for anything in particular?" he said coldly.

"Weapons."

"You'll find a gun case on the other side of the table. There should be a rifle and a shotgun in it."

"We already have those."

"Who the hell *are* you?"

"Major von Holbach, German East African Protective Force. This is Sergeant Karstedt."

The sergeant was dark and square and looked like a provincial inn-keeper. Both men acted and moved with deliberate composure. They seemed to be as familiar with the ground as Kendon.

He finished dressing and found he was keeping his temper with difficulty. "I told you what weapons I had. What else do you want?"

Von Holbach did not bother to reply. He tipped over the cot and Karstedt pushed it to the far wall of the tent. He dragged in two safari chairs and the table from outside.

In the first grey light of dawn the Germans looked as though they had recently been through a sandstorm. Every time they moved their clothes gave off small puffs of dust.

"Fetch the other one," von Holbach said.

Karstedt stepped outside and issued a series of orders. A few minutes later two German *askaris*, also wearing South African uniform, pushed Storey into the tent.

"Sit!" von Holbach ordered.

"I don't take orders from Germans," Storey said.

Von Holbach settled behind the folding table. "When your hip begins to hurt please use the chair."

"As an American citizen, I must protest . . ." Kendon began.

"As an American citizen you are working for the British in a theatre of war. I could shoot you out of hand."

"You're wearing South African uniforms. *You* could be shot for that," Storey said.

"By whom? You?" Von Holbach rose. "Let us not talk of rights. We're wasting time. First there is some personal business." He motioned to Karstedt, who left the tent. When he returned he was followed by two *askaris* who carried an elderly, emaciated tribesman on a stretcher. The man looked like a collection of bones in a dusty brown leather bag.

"He won't live beyond this evening," von Holbach said. "When he dies, I wish you to remember that you killed him."

"Don't talk nonsense!" Kendon said.

"Not only him, but twelve other members of his tribal group and about forty head of cattle."

"He's a Nandi," Storey said. "Why would I want to kill a Nandi?"

"They were trekking with their cattle to the waterhole down there," von Holbach said. "Their scouts came back and said the water was poisoned, so they tried to drive their cattle back across the desert. Some got through, some died. Why would you want to kill a Nandi? You didn't. You wanted to kill a German patrol, like us."

"No one would have been poisoned," Storey said angrily.

Von Holbach drew back his hand and struck him across the mouth. He staggered and would have fallen if Kendon had not grabbed him.

"That's a hell of a thing to do to an old man!" Kendon said.

"It's a hell of a thing poisoning water-holes!" von Holbach said. "I come from German South West. We lived near the Kalahari

212

before the war drove us out. In all my life there, I never heard of anyone poisoning a waterhole."

"I tell you it wasn't poisoned!" Storey said.

Von Holbach said contemptuously: "I saw the carcasses myself. Animals and birds that had died after drinking the water. Don't bother to lie."

"Dead game. Yes. Cigar and my gun-boy shot them. To make it look as though the water was poisoned."

Von Holbach's face darkened with anger. "Poison or no poison, you knew we had been using that waterhole on and off. You knew we wouldn't drink. You hoped we'd die of thirst!"

For a moment Kendon thought he was going to shoot Storey, then the old man said, "I didn't know. I guessed."

Von Holbach stared at him for some moments, then said, "All right. You didn't put poison in the water. But you still killed a dozen Nandi. Congratulations." He pointed to the old man on the stretcher. "Take him out. Let him die in peace."

The heat in the tent was fierce. Kendon and Storey had been alone for some hours. A Ger-

213

man *askari* stood near the tent opening. Kendon had studied him briefly but without hope. There was an efficiency about these native troops that the British *askaris* lacked. Brent had dominated his men by fear, these were part of a team.

Before von Holbach left he had said, "Don't try to escape, Kendon. *You* may manage it, we can't be everywhere at once. But not Storey. He can't run fast enough and if you go, we'll shoot him. After what he did there is not a single one of my *askaris* who would hesitate."

He and Storey had not talked much. The old man had sat rigidly in his chair looking past Kendon into some other world and dabbing occasionally at the trickle of blood in the corner of his mouth. And Kendon, with the picture in his mind of the dying Nandi, of the bodies lying out in the scrub desert under the terrible sun, found that he had little to say to the Colonel.

Food was brought at mid-morning. Storey ignored his. Kendon ate sparingly. Then he said, "He knew about your injury." Storey nodded. "In fact, he knew all about you. And me. Knew I was American. He could have picked it by the accent, I guess, but it didn't sound like that. And he knew it was you who had been to the waterhole."

Storey said nothing.

"Why didn't you tell me what you were doing?"

"Why should I?"

"It was a hell of a thing to do!"

"Look," Storey said, suddenly shaking with anger. "This isn't your war! What the hell has it got to do with you? It was something *I* could do! It was *my* contribution!"

Von Holbach came at noon. He ordered Storey to stay where he was, but called Kendon outside. It was a relief to stand on the Escarpment in the slight breeze. Only then did Kendon realize fully how efficient von Holbach was. His tent and the tents of his score of *askaris* were pitched in precisely the same places Brent had pitched his. Not a coolie, not a Jemadar, would consider von Holbach and his men to be other than Empire troops.

The German seemed to read his thoughts. "Tell me, has Brent recovered?" he said.

"You know about Brent?" Kendon asked, unwillingly.

"We made some inquiries about him after he had beaten your chief stone-mason."

"How did you know about that?"

"By reading your telegrams. Seems Brent's never been able to keep his hands off black men. He nearly beat an *askari* to death in Mombasa. Did *you* know that? There was a court martial but Brent said the man had struck him first. He was reduced from major to captain."

He was leading the way towards the top of the Escarpment. "By the way, my congratulations. I studied engineering at Leipzig. Mechanical, not civil, but even so I can appreciate the work you have done on the incline." Kendon did not respond. After they had been climbing for a while he said, "You say you've been watching us?"

"Ja. Didn't you ever wonder why you were not being blown up like the main line?"

"We thought you couldn't get across the desert."

"Even after you'd found the waterhole and the body?"

"Was he one of yours? There was nothing left of the body to tell who it had been. The horse worried us."

"Storey must have guessed."

"Yes. He thought it might have been a lion or—"

"There was a lion at the waterhole yesterday. Karstedt wounded it."

"There were two originally. The other one is dead."

"I know."

"You seem to know everything!" In spite of himself, he was responding to von Holbach. "Tell me, if you could get as close to us as the waterhole, why *haven't* you blown us up?"

"Why should we? We want the line ourselves. If the lions had given you much more trouble we would even have helped you shoot them. We wanted the line built. But you were too efficient. You went too fast for us. You had to be slowed down."

Kendon looked at him sharply, but at that moment they came to the top of the Escarpment. Above the start of Gradient A he could make out the bulky figure of Karstedt lying in the grass. He held binoculars.

"Any movement on the plain?" von Holbach asked in German as they reached him.

"Nothing new."

An *askari* came up the Escarpment at the double and handed von Holbach a telegram

He read it and passed it to Kendon: a special train was due to come through from Nairobi at 1800 hours.

"A special train?"

"The one you asked for," von Holbach said. "I took the liberty of sending a telegram on your behalf to say that the cable incline was tested and ready."

"You sent—!"

"Also on Colonel Robertson's behalf. Our information is that Smuts puts great trust in you both."

"We only completed Gradient B yesterday! It hasn't been tested . . ."

Von Holbach shrugged. "Every operation has one or two risks."

"Wait a minute! You're not seriously going to take a train down? Anything might happen!"

"I can assure you I am quite serious."

"But this 'special' will be a Red Cross train. It'll have doctors and nurses aboard."

"Our information is that it will contain troops. Reinforcements. Smuts is not going to allow Kisimi to fall if he can help it."

". . . Medical supplies . . . food . . . you can't risk . . ."

"That will depend on how well you've built."

Kendon glanced down the slope. The coolies were at work tree-felling, building up piles of fuel, dragging the supplies on the Mid-Level to the loading platforms at the top of Gradient B. Already some of the trucks were loaded with rafts and boats. He could even make out Jemadar Singh far down the slope doing his normal work. It suddenly struck him that everything was going much as it would have gone had he still been in charge, and he realized that von Holbach had brought him to the Escarpment to preserve just such an appearance of normality. What could be more normal than for Sahib Kendon to be seen talking with an Allied Officer?

He said abruptly, "If you're right and this train is loaded with troops and not Red Cross personnel, why should *you* want to take it down?"

"We don't," von Holbach said. "That's why I'm so delighted to come across an engineer of your calibre. *We* are going to be the guinea pigs on your Gradient B. *We* are going into Kisimi."

"You? You'll never make it!"

"Think about it. Who is going to suspect a

train coming from this direction, especially when Kisimi has been warned to expect it?"

"Colonel Robertson for one."

"Not after you send this telegram on to him by runner with a note saying Gradient B has been tested."

"What about the troops in Kisimi? They'll soon find you out."

"Why should they? I speak English. I was at school in South Africa. I agree that after a time they might become suspicious of Karstedt and the *askaris*. But we don't need much time. I don't think there will be any trouble."

Kendon felt a sudden chill. "The train that's coming—what about that?"

"All we want is the locomotive. We'll use those trucks . . ." he pointed to the loaded wagons on the Mid-Level.

"You'll never get the locomotive without—"

"I think I know my job better than you. We'll stop the train—there are a dozen places within twenty kilometres where it can be done. Then we will detach the locomotive."

"Without loss of life?"

Von Holbach was at the end of his patience. "I give no guarantees. My men will be covering the train with machine-guns."

"But what if it *is* a Red Cross train? What if your information is wrong?" Kendon persisted.

"My information is excellent."

"But what if—"

"War makes certain things inevitable."

"Of course they'll blow the train," Storey said. "They're not playing children's games. And he's right, it will be easy to detach the locomotive. They're in the right uniforms. The train will stop for them. They'll have their machine-guns hidden in the *nyika* to make everyone in the coaches keep their heads down. They can do it, all right. First the train, and then they'll get into Kisimi and blow the ammunition dump."

"You make it sound simple."

"There's a formula for this kind of action. I saw it in the Boer War. The enemy will start a barrage as von Holbach's men are due to go in. The place will be chaotic. I can't see anyone noticing them, let alone asking what they're doing. They'll cut Kisimi off completely and then wait for their own people to come in from the perimeter and take the place."

Kendon nervously rubbed his hand on the back of his neck. Things were happening too fast. They were giving him no time to think, to make plans. Von Holbach and Karstedt had walked him about the Escarpment and the camp, allowing him to be seen. He had thought of alternative escape plans: getting to the telegraph hut to send off a message; sending Jemadar Singh with word to Colonel Robertson. But the telegraph hut was under guard and there was never any chance to speak privately with the Jemadar. In any case, there was always the German threat against Storey.

He had been returned to his tent at three o'clock in the afternoon, three hours before the special train was due, and for the first time was able to sit down with Storey and analyse the Germans' intentions.

It was a simple question of transposition: instead of a British train being lowered down the cable incline and making its way to the lake shore, it would be a German train. Instead of containing British troops (if von Holbach was right), it would contain German native troops dressed as British native troops and a German officer and sergeant dressed as South Africans. The train would only travel after dark. There would be no reason for Robertson to suspect anything. If the message was to be left until the last minute, as von Holbach planned, Robertson would hardly have time to digest it before the train would be moving along his track. Kendon could visualize it clearly: at the lake shore they would simply take three or four native fishing boats, or perhaps the small rowing boats which formed the ferry service and which he himself had used. And then . . . by the time anyone in Kisimi realized the new arrivals were Germans and not South Africans, everything would be over.

# 13

THE young lion lay beneath a tangled mass of thorns on top of a high bank overlooking the track. Instinct had brought it back this far. It lay awkwardly because it could not stretch out its left front leg which had stiffened badly from the second joint up to the shoulder.

Since its older companion had left the waterhole the young lion had not fared well. It had made several kills but had missed three times as many. In desperation it had attacked a rhino and had been badly knocked about.

It had taken two days to recover from that experience and was about to go out in search of food again when it had scented man. It had worked its way deep into the thick thorn cover that surrounded the waterhole and watched the arrival of a party of horsemen. They had drawn up short of the water. None drank. The horses had begun to fight their way towards the water hole. One of the men had shouted and the riders had dismounted and dragged their mounts away. They had moved off towards the railway line, passing close to the lion's hide. It had waited until the last man had passed before it began its pattern of attack.

But things had gone badly wrong. Even before it had cleared the thorn scrub it became aware that there was another rider. The man had seen the animal and fired. The bullet had caught the lion just above the second joint of its left leg, fracturing the bone. It had given a roar of pain and rage and flung itself into thick thornbush.

It had waited there until all sounds and all scent of man had vanished then it had made its way towards the railway line. It had travelled very slowly because of the pain in its leg.

That had been twenty-four hours ago. Now, although the bleeding had stopped, the leg had stiffened. Instinct had brought the lion back to the railway line. Later, when it grew dark, it would travel farther. Although it had no memory of the cave, it was aware of a feeling of safety in the direction it was taking.

Jemadar Ragbir Singh told himself that whatever was happening, it was not his business. Although he had lived in British East Africa for nearly twenty years he had not identified himself with the country. He never thought of himself as African. When he had needed a wife he had sent back to the Punjab for her. The Jemadar was a snob. He considered all coolies and many Europeans to be beneath him. Tribesmen he regarded as little more than animals. The Jemadar had come a long way: he could read, he could write, he served only one man, Sahib Kendon. He had that most precious thing of all: dignity.

*Was* it his business? By acting, would he not put himself in danger for the sake of other people who were not even Punjabis?

And yet, when he thought of the day's events, he quivered with indignation. That morning he had received a report that someone was or had been near the explosives hut. When he got there he found the padlock broken and the door hanging open. The hut was empty. He had been on his way to report to Kendon when he had been stopped by a black soldier. The black soldier had told Jemadar Ragbir Singh to clear off.

He had ignored the fellow, naturally, and had tried to get to the sahib's tent by another route. This time he had come upon a white soldier talking with Karim Ram. That had been an amazing sight. Karim Ram had seen him and said something to the soldier, who had ordered the Jemadar to follow him. He had told the Jemadar that Sahib Kendon was feeling sick and that he should get the men to work as usual. But, he had replied, if the sahib was sick then he, the Jemadar, would look after him. That was his business. In any case, he had the night report to give.

And then the most terrible thing had happened. In full sight of the work force, Karim Ram had taken him by the collar and the seat of his trousers and pitched him into the dust. His *puggaree* had come off and his hair had been fouled. Nothing like it had happened to him in all his life before.

The strange thing was that much of his fear of Ram had evaporated. It seemed that the moment the huge Bengali had placed his hands on Singh he had released his fear. So that when the Jemadar decided to act it was from a mixture of motives of which personal pride was the strongest.

In the hottest part of the day when the coolies were resting in the shade before starting the afternoon shift, he made his way along a dry gully that cut down at an angle to the plain. The gully was just deep enough to hide him. He was working out what he would tell the British Colonel. He would explain about the explosives hut, of course, and perhaps he might say he had seen Ram there. He would not actually say when. And he would tell him about Sahib Kendon's sickness and how the soldiers had kept him from the tent. As he made his way down the Escarpment he became more and more self-pitying, more filled with injured pride. He would tell the Colonel how his night report had been taken away from him . . . how he had been ordered to work by . . .

A rifle muzzle pointed at him from the middle of a bush. For a moment he was paralysed with shock, then his hands shot skyward. The bush moved and a British officer stepped from behind its branches.

"Get over there!" the officer ordered, indicating the high bank of the gully.

There was something familiar about him. And then the Jemadar realized who he was. Although he was thinner and his dead white face bore a livid weal across one cheek, Singh knew him as the officer who had been attacked by the lion, the one who had thrashed Karim Ram.

A white sergeant and two dozen British *askaris* rose from the ground behind him.

Two of them grabbed the Jemadar and hustled him into the cover of the bush.

"I know you," Brent said. "You're Ṣahib Kendon's man." The Jemadar nodded. He was afraid of Brent. "Is the food train in yet?" Singh shook his head. "Good. Sergeant!"

"Sir?"

"I want you to detail one of your men to watch this man . . . no, wait a minute. I think we'll take him. Make an example of him if the coolies start trouble."

"Sahib!" Singh said. "Sahib, there is something you must know . . ."

Kendon stood at the tent flap and called to the German *askari*. The soldier was crouched in the grass, pretending that he wasn't guarding the tent. Kendon called again and he looked up. He beckoned, but the *askari* shook his head. Kendon turned to Storey, who was lying on the cot. "He won't come."

"Try again!"

Ever since he had decided that Storey's life was not worth a whole town, he had tried to keep the thought of what might happen out of his mind. Then Storey himself had said,

"You can't let a whole town go down!" He said it as though it were Kendon's fault.

It was then they had decided to kill the *askari*. Storey had taken off his yellow silk scarf, knotted it and said, "That's how the dacoits did it." Kendon had taken the scarf unwillingly, telling himself there was no alternative.

He called again, more urgently: "The old man very sick!" The *askari* just stared at him.

He made a turning motion with his hand near his head and pointed to the tent. Storey groaned loudly.

The *askari* rose and came towards him. He motioned with the rifle for Kendon to go to the opposite side of the cot, and bent forward to look at Storey. From where he stood, Kendon could see no way of getting the scarf around the African's neck. Suddenly Storey reached up and grabbed the rifle, jerking the *askari* down on top of him. Kendon launched himself. There was a clawing mêlée. The rifle fell free. As he reached for it, Kendon felt hands grip his throat. Then there was the sound of a blow and the grip loosened. He looked up to see Jemadar Singh, holding a heavy stick in his hands. The *askari* lay on the ground.

"How the hell did you get here?" Kendon said.

There was silence as the Jemadar tried to put his thoughts in order.

"Come on, man!"

"Sahib, it not being easy to explain. . . ."

It reminded Kendon of the morning report. Everything had to be gone through in order. Singh started with his discovery of the dynamite store and his attempt to report that the door was off its hinges. He went on to the incident with Karim Ram and how he decided something was wrong and had been on his way to Colonel Robertson when Brent had stopped him.

"Captain Brent!" Kendon said, startled.

The Jemadar described the livid scars and felt his stomach heave.

"How did he know about the Germans?" Kendon asked.

Singh explained that Brent had not known, that he had come out of Kisimi with his original party of soldiers to loot the coolies' food train.

"What!"

"He going to take all the food, sahib. He say they starving in Kisimi. He going to make the coolies carry it. If they objecting he say he

231

going to shoot me for an example." He shivered.

"Then you told him what was happening here?"

"Yes, sahib." He held up a finger and they heard a sudden patter of rifle shots. "That is Captain now."

Kendon ran outside, followed by Storey and Singh. In the distance he could see a group of German *askaris* running towards the summit. There were more shots. A man fell. The others took cover.

The Jemadar explained rapidly that Brent had planned to come up the Escarpment through the uncut timber. He had sent Singh up to report his movements to Kendon.

"Von Holbach won't give up this easily," Kendon said.

"He'll blow the whole train now," Storey said. "The engine too. Just to stop them."

Kendon turned to Singh. "Find Captain Brent. Tell him a train is coming from Nairobi. Tell him that the Germans are going to try to blow it up. Colonel Storey and I will take the trolley and go up the line and stop the train."

The Jemadar did not fancy going back over the top of the Escarpment.

"Sahib—"

"Not now! Get going!" Reluctantly the Jemadar left the tent.

Kendon and Storey lifted the dead *askari*'s body and placed it out of sight, covering it with the cot. Then they looked at each other. The firing was coming in single shots now.

"I'd slow you down," Storey said. "I'll be all right here." He picked up the carbine.

Kendon hesitated. "I'll come back for you."

"Yes."

He went out of the tent into the late afternoon. Great thunderheads were building up and the heat was severe. He knew he must be conspicuous, but there was nothing he could do about it. In any case, the firing was much higher up the slope. Half-way down he realized he was holding the Jemadar's heavy stick. It was better than nothing. His direction took him past the dynamite store with its door hanging off the hinges. He ran on. The telegraph hut was deserted. He felt a surge of hope. He went inside. The instruments were smashed, the wires cut. He ran towards the track. All the way down he had been watching for the trolley, but had not seen it. He stopped at the small siding where the trains had been unloaded but it wasn't there. He went on down the line towards the water tank. He had given orders that one trolley was always to be kept at the tank, but there was nothing.

He was now certain that somewhere along the track there was either von Holbach or Karstedt with a great deal of dynamite and quick-burning fuse. He tried to put himself into von Holbach's mind. It was obvious he wouldn't want to blow the train anywhere near the Escarpment. Where then? A map of the track unreeled itself in his head. About two miles farther on there was a high cutting. If he were doing the job he'd try to blow the train and the cutting at the same time. Anyone who wasn't killed in the explosion would be buried under tons of rock and dirt. He began to run again.

The lion had been watching the man for nearly an hour, waiting for the opportunity to attack. It had not moved from its place among the thorns on top of the cutting. The sun slanted through the thin leaves making a dappled pattern on the grass. The lion's body blended perfectly with its background. But even had it been lying out in the open it is doubtful if the man would have seen it. He was intent on his work. He was using a short steel bar and a heavy hammer to drive a series of holes into the walls of the cutting. He worked without a break, moving from one hole to the next, testing it for depth, then pushing in the bundles of dynamite sticks wrapped in threes. He used himself mercilessly. The sweat dripped from his body making patterns in the dust of the cutting. The smell of his hot body was strong in the lion's nostrils. Once, the man stopped and moved away from the cutting wall, and the lion's muscles tensed and the pain in its left leg vanished, but the man walked some distance up the line to a trolley and lifted a canvas water bottle to his lips. Then he splashed some of the water on his head and shoulders. The lion smelled the water and started to rise. The man put down the water bottle and returned to the work on the cutting walls. The lion subsided. It had taken the animal a long time to learn the one cardinal factor upon which its life would depend: patience.

Kendon saw the trolley. It was in the place he had expected, standing in the middle of the *nyika*. No attempt had been made to hide it. Their confidence did not escape him.

So far his mind had been on finding the place where the train was to be blown and on how to keep his legs moving quickly. He had found the place: what now? Instinctively, he swerved off the track and hid in a grassy patch that formed a tiny glade in the thorn. His heart was pounding, his breath coming in harsh gusts. Whatever he was to do, it could not be done without thought.

He was on the left side of the cutting just where the walls began to rise. The cutting itself was in the shape of a bow so he could not see into it from where he was, but could hear the sound of hammering. He decided to try and work his way through the *nyika* to the top of the cutting so he could look down into it.

It took him more than ten minutes to move thirty yards. Each forward movement was arrested by the thorns that caught in his clothing. Some broke off under pressure, others fastened more tightly into the tough khaki. He would have to stop and remove each thorn before it lacerated his flesh. At the top the thorn had been hacked away when the cutting was built and the ground was par-

236

tially clear. He pulled himself along on his elbows until he was able to see over the edge. He found himself looking down on Karim Ram.

The Bengali had completed the required number of holes and was crouching over a series of fuse wires. For a moment Kendon was too astonished to make sense of what he was seeing, then he began to work things out. He knew now how the Germans had kept watch on the railway and he knew why the stone-masons had worked so badly. He wondered how long Ram had been working for them, and then wondered how he was going to stop him blowing the line. A stick was not enough. Ram would take it away from him and then break him in two. But if he could use the advantage of height, say by dislodging a rock . . . He looked about him. He did not see a rock, but there was a discarded wooden sleeper. The thorn had already grown over it but he might be able to move it to the top of the wall. If he could stand it upright and tip it over it would gather enough speed through the drop of twelve feet to knock down a rhino.

He turned and began to wriggle into the thorn. At that moment he heard a low growl.

The lion had risen from its place under the tree fifteen yards away and was standing, looking at him.

Karim Ram had also heard the growl and turned. The two men and the lion stood perfectly still. The lion could see the men; the men could see the lion and each other. Slowly the lion's body dropped into a crouch. For the briefest moment Kendon and Karim Ram were united in their fear. Then in the same instant they turned to run. The motion of Kendon's body gathered the branches and thorn around him. He was able to move for only a second, then he was held fast. Karim Ram had no such impediment. He ran heavily along the track to the rifle that lay on the trolley. Kendon was aware of a yellow blur passing him as the lion leapt down the side of the cutting, following the moving figure.

It took him nearly twenty minutes to free himself. For some of that time he tried to blot out the sounds from below. He would never know exactly what happened during the first five minutes, but the sounds had indicated that Ram was not dying without a fight. Then the noises had ceased. By the time he had freed himself and moved to the edge of the cutting again all that remained of the struggle was a piece of torn clothing and an area of cut-up earth.

He told himself that if Storey were there, or if he had a rifle, he would have gone into the thorn after Ram; but they were rationalizations. He had been frightened when the lion had tried to attack in the railway truck, but when the thorns had gripped him and the lion had flattened to the ground, he had known what real terror was.

He was still standing at the top of the cutting when he heard the whistle of a train. It was less than a mile away, the smoke-smudge black against the towering clouds. He climbed down into the cutting and checked the fuses Ram had laid. None had been wired up. He ran to the mouth of the cutting and on down the track towards the train.

"What the hell are you playing at?" a voice cried. A Lieut. Colonel jumped down on to the track. He held a revolver.

Kendon had brought the train to a halt by waving his shirt. The Colonel stared at the lacework of thin red lines that covered his chest and back. Then he shouted: "I'll give you five seconds to get off the line!" He was a big man with a dark moustache and hair that brushed the collar of his tunic.

"Don't be a damned fool! I want to talk to you!"

"Well! At least you're not a Hun!"

Kendon looked past him at an Indian soldier who had jumped on to the track and started to run away from the train. The Colonel whirled. "Come on!" he yelled. "Where the hell are you? Shoot the bugger!" The Indian was about forty yards from the track when rifle barrels poked from the train. There was a ragged volley. The soldier went on running. "For Christ's *sake!*" the Colonel shouted.

Farther down the train another soldier began to clamber out of a window.

"Stop that man!" the Colonel shouted.

There was another volley and the running soldier crashed to the ground. The second Indian, half out of the window, began to scramble back. A dozen or more heavily-bearded Sikhs jumped from the train and stood facing it with fixed bayonets.

"Now, sir, what the hell are *you* up to?"

Briefly, Kendon told him. The Colonel did not put away his revolver. "Show me," he ordered. They walked back into the cutting.

Half an hour later the train began to move towards Railhead. Kendon and the Colonel, who had introduced himself as Harris of the 101st Grenadiers, were standing on the footplate. After he had seen the dynamite and fuses, Harris had put away his gun. "Dearie me," he had said, "what a nasty mess that would have made."

Then Kendon told him exactly what had been happening. He listened without comment. Then he said: "I know Brent. This food business is his own idea. There isn't an officer in Kisimi who'd be foolish enough to jeopardize the railway. They know it's their only way out. I suppose Brent thought that if he turned up with food someone would pin a medal on him."

"Whatever brought him, he's here."

Harris nodded. "I don't like . . . what do you call them in your country? Grandstand players?"

"We'd be in bad shape without him."

"Worse than you think. My chaps would soil themselves if I even suggested fighting. They've been trying to leave the train at every water stop since Nairobi. Had to shoot one or two *pour encourager*, as you might say."

"Why the hell send them, then?"

"They're all we've got: Madrassis, 13th Rajputs, some Pioneers. Horribly chewed up by the Hun at Tanga and been good for nothing ever since. No, they haven't come to fight at all, just to bear stretchers, row boats, help with the evacuation."

"But I thought Smuts was going to hold Kisimi!"

"Haven't you heard? Von Lettow-Vorbeck's mauled the South Africans on the Masai steppes. Every available man has been sent down there in case there's a breakthrough. There's no hope of holding Kisimi. All we can do is try to get as many out as possible."

In the late afternoon the noise on the Escarpment was prodigious. Men were shouting, the steam winch at the top of Gradient B was chuffing, the brake drums at the top of Gradient A were whining, coaches were being lowered, trucks in ballast were coming up as counter-weights, everywhere was movement; and every now and then came the crack of a rifle.

Brent and his *askaris* had driven the Germans away from the cable incline and they had taken positions deep in the uncut timber on the upper slope. The British troops were occupying positions along the track, using piles of cut timber as firing posts. But the Germans were free to move to higher ground. This one or two of them had done and, although they were more than five hundred yards from the Mid-Level, their bullets occasionally found a target.

Harris and Kendon were on the Mid-Level in the shelter of a truck. Farther down the slope was the body of a coolie who had been shot when he was helping to move the truck to the waiting carrier at the loading point. Now another truck was being pushed to the loading point, the unwilling coolies urged on by Jemadar Singh who had his cane *lathi* to support him.

Harris ran his fingers through his hair. "It's going to take bloody days like this!"

When his train had reached the top of the Escarpment and they heard the increased barrage from the German field-guns on the Kisimi perimeter they had known there was going to be no time for testing: the carriers and the cable winches on Gradient B were going to have to do it right the first time. But the sniping was slowing things down.

They saw Brent, his riding-crop flicking up and down, shout at a dozen coolies who were hiding in the lee of a truck. He began to hit out. The coolies tried to stay in safety but he drew his revolver and fired over their heads. They emerged reluctantly and began to push the truck to the loading point.

Brent came towards them and saluted Harris, in the open, purposely exposing himself to the sniper fire.

"My chaps won't stand much more of this," Harris said.

"I've never come across a good Madrassi," Brent said.

"All depends on the way you treat them—but you'd know all about that." Brent stared at Harris with his pale eyes. There was not a flicker to show he might have understood the words' implication. "I want you to take a couple of men and try to get above the snipers."

"They're hidden in the trees. We really need a class shot."

"What about Storey?" Kendon said suddenly. "He's supposed to be the best shot in East Africa. Even if he couldn't get above them he might be able to pin down von Holbach and Karstedt."

"He's worse than useless," Brent said.

"That's not true!"

"There's no time for chat!" Harris said. "Get him up there. Carry him, if you have to!"

Kendon watched Brent's short square figure duck out from under the truck, and walk up Gradient B. He stopped and Kendon saw Storey stand up from his place behind a pile of cut wood. Brent once more began to climb. He went too fast for Storey and the old man struggled to keep up. Brent marched as though he was leading a regiment.

"Bloody fool!" Harris said.

Brent added one or two *askaris* to his small force and then they left the tracks and began to work their way into the timber high up on the right-hand slope. Kendon lost sight of them, then there was renewed firing. This time it was not static. The direction from whch it was coming began to shift. The Germans were being driven farther away across the face of the Escarpment. After fifteen minutes he realized the firing had almost stopped.

"You'd better get your contraption working," Harris said.

Dusk had enveloped the Escarpment. The rifle fire came in single separate shots at infrequent intervals. But the German bombardment at Kisimi was reaching a climax. It seemed part of another world, nothing to do with the Escarpment. On the Mid-Level and along the sides of Gradient B the gangs of coolies were squatting. A silence had fallen over them. They watched, saying nothing. The steam winch began to clank and puff, the Howard clips to knock: slowly the first carrier with a freight truck loaded with boats and rafts, began the first descent of the new gradient. Kendon, Harris, Jemadar Singh, and Marston, the grey-haired engine driver who had brought the troop train from Nairobi, were all standing at the steam winch. Kendon, his hands on the brake levers, was tense. Harris said something, but he did not hear. He was part of the whole huge structure. As the carrier fell away below him he experienced a great surge of emotion. Robertson had said it wouldn't work. Robertson was wrong.

After the first carrier had reached the bottom safely, the operation went smoothly: first the freight trucks then the troop coaches went swaying down on to the plain. It was dark by the time the last coach had gone.

The train now stood on the plain with its boats and rafts and its three-hundred stretcher bearers. But it had no life, without its locomotive it was useless. Kendon had kept the engine until last. It was the smallest shunting engine that could be found in Nairobi, but even so it weighed more than thirty tons. Steam was up and it was ready for use the moment it reached the plain.

A gang of coolies pushed it on to a specially reinforced carrier. Marston and Simmonds, the ruddy-faced young fireman, stood by watching. The wheels were secured.

"Might be safer walking," Kendon said.

"May as well ride," Marston said. "What about you, Jack?"

"Too bloody dark for walking," Simmonds said.

Kendon hesitated. "Get aboard then."

The locomotive began its descent. Looking down, from the vantage point on the Mid-Level, it was a strange sight. Along the track, pitch torches were burning. Everything else was shadowy, black-and-orange. The locomotive was beginning to lose its sharp outlines and became a great shining mass of metal dropping down into the flickering void.

And then it began to shake. Kendon saw it too late. The flames of the torches were causing great dancing shadows. The shake turned into a dreadful swaying motion. It was moving too quickly. The weight was pulling the cable out too fast for the winch. The swaying increased. He could see the railbed itself begin to move. He recalled Robertson talking about lateral stability. That was the trouble now. There was no lateral stability. He realized he should have used wider sleepers. He dragged on the check lever but the cable continued to pull out. The weight of the locomotive, added to the motion it had created, was too much to hold. The cable stretched. The carrier bucked to one side. The cable snapped and the locomotive plunged sideways off the track and began to roll down the slope, spewing out steam and red-hot cinders.

"**Y**OU'D need a mobile crane," Colonel Robertson said. "Even then it would be a waste of time. That thing's finished." They were standing near the dead locomotive. Kendon looked up and saw the scar it had left on the hillside, then his eyes were drawn back to the engine. It lay on its side, battered and scratched, its pipes burst, twisted, broken, its boiler dented, the cab crushed down on to the footplate. That was where they had found Marston, crumpled almost beyond recognition. Although they had searched all night they had only discovered the second body in the early dawn. And as they searched they had heard the guns at Kisimi. The bombardment had lasted nearly fourteen hours.

He turned away and began to climb Gradient B. Half-way up, two lengths of steel had been torn away by the engine.

"Where are you going?" Robertson said. He had not mentioned lateral stability, had not so much as hinted at the fact that his advice had been ignored, but his expression was bleak.

Kendon was numb. He felt disorientated, almost unaware of where he was or what he was doing.

"You can't just walk away from it!" Robertson shouted after him. "This was *yours*!"

But he went on walking up the slope, leaving the Colonel standing near the broken engine.

Storey was on the Mid-Level. His face was grey with fatigue and he held his heavy rifle. Kendon stood at the winch and looked down on to the plain. The train was ready and waiting but its motive power was gone.

After a moment Storey said, "We weren't wrong!"

"We?"

"It's wartime. You try things in wartime. Sometimes they work . . ."

"And sometimes they don't."

"Don't be a fool! Of course it's worked. Not completely, but it's bloody worked! You've done what you said you'd do. You've put a train down there!"

"But nothing to pull it with. We can get the trucks to the lake all right. It's a down grade all the way. That's not the problem. But how do we bring the wounded out? How do we pull them back to the Escarpment without an engine?"

As he spoke they heard a shot. The bullet struck the winch handle some inches in front of him. Then Harris's voice shouted, "Take cover!" All over the slope the coolies began to scatter. Storey and Kendon crouched behind the winch.

"There's one way of getting them back," Storey said. "My old engine in Kisimi."

"What old engine?"

"That's if it hasn't been blown to pieces. Harry Goodman can get it moving."

"*What engine?*"

"My old traction engine!"

"The monument?"

"It'd pull your coaches back if you could get it across the lake."

Kendon stared at him. He saw again, in his mind's eye, the piece of polished Victorian machinery that stood in the "public gardens". If they could get it across the lake it should be able to pull a train to the base of the Escarpment. Then if he got the tracks on Gradient B relaid. . . .

Harris came up to them. "There's something I've got to talk to you about," Kendon said.

"Later. Now there's only one thing to concentrate on: we've got to get water down to the plain. I'm not even worried about the food, just water. Otherwise we'll have no stretcher bearers and no one to row us across the lake." He hurried away, calling over his shoulder, "Storey, I want you!"

All that day the German patrol kept up an intermittent fire. They were hidden deep in the bush, too deep to do much damage. Harris, Storey, Brent and Miller, each with two or three *askaris*, penetrated the bush from time to time and poured in rifle fire.

At first the coolies refused to work. Nothing in their contracts called for being shot at while laying steel. But when Kendon recklessly exposed himself to the German rifles and they had seen the effect of Harris's pursuit, they reluctantly emerged.

As the day passed, the Germans changed their tactics and concentrated their fire on the coaches and trucks at the foot of the Escarpment. Kendon knew that the Indians cooped up in the coaches must be having a grim time. Harris hadn't dared to let them out because he hadn't enough men to prevent them trying to escape.

\ Half-way through the afternoon Harris, hurrying as usual, called to Kendon: "We'll meet at eighteen hundred hours on the Mid-Level. I've told Robertson."

"What about Storey? I haven't seen him."

"Don't worry about Storey. He's all right."

By six o'clock, when Harris, Kendon and Robertson met, the two sections of buckled track on Gradient B were relaid and two water trucks with their huge tanks stood at the top of Gradient A waiting to be lowered on the funicular section. A heavy mist had begun to cover the summit of the Escarpment and the air was saturated with humidity.

"We have to move at dusk," Harris said. "It's going to take the whole night to cross the lake." He turned to Robertson. "Kendon says it's a down gradient the whole way to the lake shore. You built it. You should know."

"He's right." It was said grudgingly. "Slight, but a down gradient."

"He says the coaches and trucks could be pushed. Is that right?"

"It's possible. But what about von Holbach's patrol?"

"I'll worry about that."

"What do you think he'll do?" Kendon said.

Harris shook his head. "Don't know. But whatever he does, we've got to go. The German field-guns will start again when it's dark. Another night of it and Kisimi might collapse. We've got to get the troops out, and the wounded—or as many of them as we can. We'll get in. That's not what's bothering me. It's how the hell we get them back."

"There's an old traction engine in Kisimi," Kendon said. "It used to belong to Storey. If we could get that working and . . ."

"Good God!" Robertson said. "You'd never get a thing like that across the lake and even if you did . . ."

"Tell me about it," Harris said.

"It's the town monument," Kendon said. "They use it every year to pull a couple of floats down the street. Means it's in some sort of order."

"Know anything about them?"

He shook his head.

"Robertson?"

"No."

"There's a policeman called Goodman who looks after it and drives it."

"I must protest!" Robertson said. "This is

another of Kendon's fantasies. Like Gradient B. I said it wouldn't work . . ."

"Wouldn't work!" Harris said. "Christ, what are you talking about? Of course it worked. It lifted three hundred men and a dozen or more trucks with boats and rafts and medical supplies down a bloody great mountain. If that isn't working, I'd like to know what is!"

"And lost an engine and two lives and . . ."

"That's enough!" Harris was white with anger. "You drawing-board wallahs don't know what war is all about! We lost two men. We're trying to save two thousand!" He turned to Kendon. "We'll try it! If it doesn't work, we'll have to walk back carrying the wounded. Which means that the Germans can bring their guns up to the lake shore and plaster us. Let's hope your traction engine will go."

The mist began to move down the slope of the mountain. It had reached the half-way point when the short twilight ended. Kendon had brought the two water trucks down Gradient A and they had been loaded on to the carriers at the top of Gradient B. Robertson was at the winch. Kendon stepped onto the second carrier. Just as Robertson was about to lower, Harris hurried up and stepped on beside him. "Got room for a little one?" he said. Kendon knew it was a gesture, but it was one he needed. They went off the edge of the Mid-Level, backwards into the dark void.

When they reached the plain, Harris went into the first of the troop coaches. Kendon followed with Jemadar Singh and the water party. In the light of a pitch torch they could see glass splinters, glistening blood, and bodies. At the end of each coach stood two Sikhs. The Madrassi troops had been ordered to lie down to escape the rifle fire. Some would never get up. Kendon wondered if they had all been killed by bullets. Then he saw the rusty red of the Sikh's bayonets.

"Let them have as much water as they can drink," Harris said. "Food will have to wait until tomorrow. Give them something to look forward to." As he spoke the German guns opened up again on the Kisimi perimeter.

By eight o'clock the troops had been watered. A thin drizzle was falling, cooling the air. "Storey and one or two *askaris* can stay here," Harris said. "Brent and his chaps will convoy us to the lake shore and then come back here."

"What about your Madrassis? They'll have to push the trucks. Won't they start deserting again?"

"Brent and his *askaris* will keep on our flanks. Anyway, I've told the Sikhs to pass the word that those guns are ours and that Kisimi will be safe by the time we get there. I also told them to pass the word that the country around here is teeming with man-eaters. We'll see what happens. You'd better take a gun."

"I'm a non-combatant."

"Don't be bloody silly! The Germans won't stop to ask questions."

Kendon accepted a revolver. It did not make him feel any better.

The trucks moved out like ghosts, only a soft click-clicking betraying their movement. There were ten open trucks and four troop coaches and Harris had allocated ten men to a truck. Each group of ten was guarded by one Sikh. They hadn't gone more than half a mile when the first Madrassi troops began to jump from the carriage windows. It was too dark to see them clearly but their running feet could be heard. Then came stabs of light in the darkness. There was a cry, then a scream. Harris, who was walking with Kendon beside one of the trucks, disappeared for some minutes and then took up his position again. "Von Holbach?" Kendon said.

"Brent."

The trucks moved on. In the four miles to the lake only six more soldiers tried to desert. At no time were the trucks fired on by the German patrol.

In the first streaks of dawn Kisimi presented a terrible sight. The main street was pitted by shell craters. Lorries and wagons lay on their sides. Dead bullocks and dead mules littered the road and one had been blown half-way through the wooden wall of a shop. Some shops had taken hits and looked like broken teeth. Many shells had burst in the lake, stunning and killing fish and these had washed up into the warm shallows adding their stench to that of the dead mules and bullocks.

It had taken Harris's force the whole night to unload the stores and water craft and to get across the lake to Kisimi. Kendon had managed to sleep for most of that time. As he stepped ashore near the ruined jetty Harris said, "You know the town. Tell me a place where we can meet."

"The hotel," Kendon said, pointing up the

street. A Red Cross flag was flying above its pock-marked exterior. Sandbags hung crazily from the upstairs balcony, which had taken a direct hit.

Harris said, "We'll start moving out the wounded as soon as we can. It'll mean a shuttle service across the lake." He looked at his watch. "Report to me outside the hotel in three hours. By then you should know what the position is with the traction engine."

"We'll need a raft, sir. A big one."

"I'll see what we can organize. You worry about your engine."

Kendon hurried to the hospital area. Some of the tents still stood, but they had been abandoned. Others had been hit and had burnt up. There was a smell of charred wood and canvas. Where Patel's shop had been, there was only a heap of rubble. As he stood, looking at the devastation, he heard the roll of heavy guns, and flinched. Then he realized it was thunder and felt the first drops of rain on his head, heavy and warm. The rain lashed down. There was no wind. It fell perpendicularly, like chain mail. One minute he had been looking over the hospital area, the next his view was abruptly cut as though someone had opened a shower above his head. The shell holes began to fill with water. The soil was like treacle.

He stumbled across the streaming earth to the main street. He entered Winslow's Hotel. Inside the door he stopped abruptly. Wounded lay everywhere; they were packed along the corridors like cigarettes in a box. They lay in the lounge, in the billiard-room, in the bar, on the staircase: everywhere there was space enough for a recumbent body.

A doctor was bending over a man near the door. "Do you know a nurse named Margaret Storey!" Kendon called. "Is she here?"

"Who?" The doctor looked up. His eyes were sunk in purple shadows. His cheeks had not seen a razor for days, perhaps weeks.

"A nurse. Miss Storey. She was down at the tents."

"Who the hell are you?" the doctor said, looking at Kendon's civilian clothing, the revolver stuck in his belt.

Wounded soldiers turned to watch them. Farther along the hotel's entrance hall several nurses looked up. The doctor had surgical scissors in one hand and a dressing in the other. He stepped over his patient and advanced on Kendon. There was an element of madness in his tired eyes.

"I said who the hell are you?"

"My name's Kendon. I came with the force to get the wounded out."

"Well, get us out, then! Get us out!"

Kendon retreated through the door. The blinding deluge had eased but the rain seemed to have settled in. It was the first cloud-burst of the new season and he knew it might rain for twenty-four hours without checking. On the other hand the clouds could break up in the afternoon and re-form the next day. He stepped out into the rain and made his way to the lake end of the street where the public gardens were situated. As he reached the path that led away from the street he saw lines of walking wounded being formed up. In front of them bobbed a flotilla of rafts and small boats.

He walked with head bent against the rain, towards the low concrete plinth on which the traction engine rested. Since the day before, he had been worrying about the vehicle's condition. The whole business was going to be difficult enough, but what if it had been hit by shell fragments or, indeed, by a shell itself? He had decided to check before finding Goodman. Now, fearing the worst, he looked up. The plinth was bare, the traction engine gone.

He stood, stupefied, for several seconds. His mind, which had carried a picture of the green and black engine with its gleaming brass work, refused to accept a blank canvas. Was he to meet Harris only to tell him the engine had vanished? He turned and ran through the rain. He asked the first six people he saw, all of them soldiers, if they had seen a traction engine. They looked at him as though he were insane. He ran on up the main street. Soldiers huddling against the shop fronts watched him curiously. Then he saw Mackenzie, the post-master. He had taken a bunch of keys from his pocket and was opening the town's one red post box outside the steel-shuttered bank. Incredibly, there were two letters in the box.

He was staring at the letters as Kendon reached him, holding them in the shelter of his coat. He looked up. "I hope they realize these will be liable to delay," he said severely.

"I'm looking for the traction engine," Kendon said.

"How do they think I'm going to get them out?"

"The town engine."

"The what?"

"The one that stands in the gardens."

"What do you want it for?" Mackenzie asked, suspiciously.

"To help get the wounded out."

"Oh. Are they evacuating the town?"

"As many as they can."

"Well, I'm not leaving."

"Do you know where it is?"

"Are you going?"

"Not unless you know where the engine is!"

"Would you take these?"

Kendon reached for the letters and the post-master looked relieved.

"Goodman took it. Yesterday. Came down with a span of bullocks and hitched them up and dragged it off."

"Oh, Jesus!" Kendon said.

"Bullocks! What the hell are you talking about?" Harris was standing in the rain outside the hotel. Water was running off his face. "I thought the thing was supposed to go by itself."

"It takes a couple of hours to get up steam," Kendon said. "Same as a railway engine."

"Where is it, then?"

"I guess that's what everyone would like to know."

"Don't just stand there, man! Find it!"

"Look, I have no status. No one wants to talk to me. Can you let me have an officer? Someone who can give orders."

"Wait here!" Harris went into the hotel, stepping over bodies. In a few moments he was back with a major's tunic. "Put that on. If anyone wants to shoot you, refer him to me. Now, what about this fellow Goodman?"

"He's the local police chief."

"Have you tried the barracks?"

"I'm on my way there now."

As he turned away he saw Margaret in the hotel doorway. She was thinner than ever and her hair and clothing were disarrayed. At first she did not seem to recognize him as she blinked into the strong light. Then her face lit up and his heart seemed to turn over.

He ran up the stairs to her. "What are you *doing* here?" she said, gripping his arm so hard he could feel her nails dig into his skin.

"I'm looking for the engine."

"What engine?"

He told her and she began to laugh. Her laughter had an edge of hysteria. He pulled her away from the doorway and they sat on a broken bench while he explained. Gradually she became quieter.

"Where could Goodman have taken it?" he asked.

"There's only one place he could hide it: the police barracks."

"Show me!" he said.

There was water everywhere now and the mud was like grease. As they hurried he briefly told her why they needed the engine. Then she asked about her father, and he reassured her.

Half a mile from the centre of the town in its own neat *boma* and with the Union Jack still flying from the flagpole, stood the police camp. It comprised a line of thatched huts painted white and a square bungalow with a black corrugated-iron roof and screened porch which was Goodman's house. On the far side a large barnlike building made of whitewashed concrete with small barred windows was the gaol. The whole place had an air of fastidious neatness. The trees were pruned, the flowerbeds tidy and weed-free and the driveway which linked each element of the compound was neatly bordered with whitewashed stones.

They ran first to the barracks but the huts were too small to contain anything as large as the engine. They went to Goodman's house, but it wasn't there.

"It has to be in the gaol if it's here at all," Kendon said.

They stumbled through the rain towards the prison building. The side facing them was a blank wall into which small windows had been let. They ran around to the far side. The prison seemed to have been hit by a German shell, but when Kendon looked more closely he saw that the main doorway had been pulled out and the rubble pushed to one side.

"Were there any prisoners?" he said.

"There usually were. Do you think they've broken out?"

They stepped over the rubble. He pointed to ropes and crowbars. The ropes were still attached to the wooden frame of the doorway. "They didn't break out. Someone broke in."

From the doorway they could see a line of cells. Each door was open. To the left of the cells and facing them was a large room with lockers around the walls. A desk, table and chairs had been pushed against the walls. In the centre of the room stood the traction engine.

It gleamed. Its paintwork was immaculate. The boiler was painted light green with bands of black and orange. The smoke-stack was black, the fly wheel green, and the spokes of the wheels orange. In a strange way, Kendon was impressed. It stood there, smelling strongly of brass polish, not a thing of beauty, but certainly of majesty. It was powerful, monolithic. It had a presence.

"It hasn't been touched," he said. "There's not a mark on it."

"Can you drive it?"

"No. We'll have to get Goodman. Where would he be?"

"I haven't seen him for days."

They searched for him through the stricken town. There had been no shelling since dawn and by noon the queues at the lake-side stretched half-way up the main street. Soldiers were bringing out some of the wounded from the hotel. Boats were coming and going. But, Kendon noticed, other soldiers who were unhurt still lay in the shelter of the buildings. They had not been formed up yet. He looked at his watch. It was nearly 2 p.m.

They ran Goodman to ground in the Kisimi Club. The officers had moved out that morning. A shell had hit one wall. Chairs were broken, tables smashed. There was broken glass everywhere. Goodman was sitting at a table against the far wall. He had a half-full bottle of Crème de Menthe in front of him.

"The last of the Mohicans," he said as they came in, pointing to the bottle and then at the empty, glass-strewn bar. He was very drunk. "Pull up a chair," he said. "Take the weight off your feet. Find a glass. Have a drop." The air in the club was heavy with moisture and he was sweating. His normally ruddy face had taken on a violent colour.

"We're trying to get the wounded out," Kendon said sharply. "We need the traction engine."

"*My* engine?"

"The *town's* engine."

"You've got a bloody hope." He raised his head and looked at them for the first time. "Hello, Margaret." Suddenly he said, "My God!" He stood up and released the button flap of his revolver holster. He pulled out the gun and pointed it at Kendon. "You bloody bastard! Impersonating a British officer!

You're not fit to clean their boots!"

"Don't be a fool," Kendon said, taking a step towards him. "I'm not trying to—"

"I'm going to put you in the bloody jug, that's what!"

"Harry, he's trying to help!"

"How dare you come in—"

Something in Kendon gave at that instant. The wall in his mind that had, throughout the months of frustration, separated rational from irrational behaviour, had worn to a fragile thinness. Now it burst, allowing his whole personality to be swept by an inchoate rage. He jumped at Goodman, flailing his arms as a child might. He hardly knew what he was doing, but it was atavistic, murderous. Goodman's sodden brain reacted too slowly. One of the flailing blows caught him on the temple and knocked him sideways across the table so he fell on his knees. Before he could get his balance Kendon had flung himself on him and ripped the revolver out of his hands, jerking so hard that the lanyard tore away.

"Don't! Don't! DON'T!"

The sounds penetrated his mind. Margaret was screaming. She was pulling at his arm with both hands. His vision cleared. Goodman was on his back, bleeding around the mouth. Kendon was holding the revolver to his ear. He had been just about to pull the trigger.

He heard Margaret sob as he drew the gun away. "It's all right," he said shakily. "I won't shoot him." She tried to return his smile but there was too much fright at the back of her eyes. He said to Goodman, "Get up!" Goodman managed to get to his feet. "Now let's talk about the engine!"

"Anyone in here?" Harris came through the door followed by four Sikhs. "They told me you were headed this way. What's the game?"

Kendon told him, briefly, what had happened. He turned to Goodman who smiled and said with drunken bravado, "How d'you do, sir? I'm Goodman. Police. This man is imper—"

"Take him outside."

"Now wait one second—"

The soldiers hustled him out. "Against the wall," Harris said.

"You're not serious!" Margaret said.

"For God's sake!" Goodman shouted as the Sikhs pushed him up against the wall of the club. "I'm British!"

The anger had left Kendon. "Harris!" he said. "You can't—"

"Wait!" Goodman called desperately. "For God's sake, wait!"

"All right. As you were, everybody," Harris said. Goodman's face was the colour of curd. His clothes were awry. Somewhere he had lost the belt of his trousers. He crouched with one hand outstretched as though to ward off the bullets, the other gripping the top of his short khaki pants. He began to cry.

At that moment there was a whine, then a crump as a shell exploded in the town. "Oh, Christ!" Harris said. "This could be the final push."

"I'm going back to the hospital," Margaret said.

As they hurried towards the police compound Goodman seemed unable to stop talking. "You should have told me," he babbled. "Should have said it was to get the wounded out. Of course I'd have helped. Who wouldn't? I know my duty . . ."

Kendon said nothing. Goodman was frightened and he did not envy him, for his fear was twofold: he was frightened of Harris on the one hand, and of the Germans on the other. The bombardment was continuing and they walked more quickly. Goodman seemed to pull his head into his tunic as though for protection.

"Must apologize about that little misunderstanding, Kendon. But you can never be too careful. You'd be surprised how often people try to impersonate officers. There was a case only last week when . . ."

Kendon remembered his attack on the man like an aftertaste of vomit in the mouth. That blind atavistic rage had never enveloped him before, not even as a child.

Harris had detailed three British soldiers to help them and now, as they stopped in front of the traction engine, one of them said, "Blimey, she's a bit of a brute, i'n't she!"

Goodman stood looking at them and at the machine and Kendon realized that his fright was not a transitory thing. He was weighing in his mind whether it would be safer to be taken by the Germans or to be part of the evacuation.

"You'll be driving!" Kendon said harshly.

"Driving?" A shell whined overhead and they all ducked.

"By the time the Germans move in they won't have left anyone alive."

"All right," Goodman muttered. "First we've got to fill the boiler."

"How much does she hold?"

"About two hundred gallons."

"How are we going to fill her?"

"There's a hosepipe in the garden."

"Where does the water come from?"

"Small reservoir on the hill. The whole camp uses it. And there are rainwater tanks."

Kendon detailed a soldier to fetch the hose. "What about fuel? What does she burn?"

"Wood."

"Got any?"

"There's a pile at the back of the barracks. But it isn't cut."

"You two," Kendon said to the remaining two soldiers. "Start cutting and don't stop! You'll never cut too much."

Goodman began to oil every moving part of the engine. When the soldier came back with a sixty-foot length of hosepipe he attached it to the tap in the gaol's ablutions block and began to fill the boiler at an inlet below the steam chest.

"How do you check the level?" Kendon asked. "Is there a dip stick?"

"There's a glass gauge on the footplate.

She's full when that reads half. Then you've got to fill the tender."

As he worked Kendon began to feel a sense of identity with the engine. There was something solid and dependable about it.

"We've got to get a fire going," Goodman said. "She takes two hours to get up enough steam to move."

All traces of drunkenness had vanished and he was working feverishly. It seemed to Kendon that he now equated safety with the engine.

"I'll see to the fire. Where are you going now?"

Goodman was at the door. "I'll have to get some steam cylinder oil. She'll seize up without it."

"I'll send one of the men."

"I've got a can at my office on Main Street. It'll be quicker for me to go."

"Don't waste time!" Kendon shouted after him.

He and the third soldier began carrying wood. They made ten trips each from the woodpile to the traction engine. Kendon opened the fire-hole door and was about to start the fire when he decided he'd better wait for Goodman. He went to collect another armful of wood. The fuel bunker on the back of the engine was full and cut wood was beginning to pile up against the wall of the gaol. He looked at his watch. Goodman had been gone more than half an hour. It should have taken him no more than fifteen minutes. Kendon felt a thrust of savage rage and began to run.

"Carry on with the wood!" he shouted as he passed the soldiers.

The rain had slackened to a drizzle but the gunfire seemed to be heavier. He could hear shells bursting in the town and answering fire on the eastern outskirts. He reached the back of the hotel. Part of the wall had been hit. Smoke was still rising and he knew it must have happened in the past few minutes. He heard cries and saw a litter of whiteclad bodies through the broken brickwork. Then he almost stepped on Goodman.

The policeman must have been coming up the slope to the compound when the shell struck. He lay on his back with his eyes wide open, staring up at the sky. Shell splinters had cut his face. Kendon dropped on to his knees and shouted urgently: "Goodman! Goodman!" He wasn't dead, but he was barely alive. Then Kendon saw that the grass was saturated with blood and Goodman's right leg was missing at the knee. He ripped off his scarf and bound it into a tourniquet around the thigh. Then he ran into the hotel for help. He was met by a mass of patients who had been in the area of the shell-burst. Some could hardly walk; others were spotted with fresh blood.

He found Margaret bending over a man, soothing him. All around others were whimpering and trying to shuffle away from the broken wall. Some were being pulled away in case the roof collapsed.

Margaret looked at him without expression. "Have you got it going?" she said.

"No. Goodman's been hit."

"Where is he?"

"Outside. It was the same shell that did all this."

"Is he alive?"

"Only just, I think."

He saw apprehension flood into her face. "Does this mean you won't be able to get the wounded out?"

"Not unless we can keep him alive. I don't know enough about the engine—and there's no time to learn."

"I'll get a doctor," she said, and fought her way through the press.

The doctor was the same one who had sent her home with Kendon on that earlier occasion. He looked twenty years older. They hurried outside and he examined Goodman. He looked up: "He's lost a lot of blood and he's in shock."

"What can you do?"

"Morphia for the shock. I'll fix a Spencer Wells clamp on the artery. I understand you want to move him. I wouldn't allow it in any other circumstances. You'll have to watch the clamp. They can slip."

"I'll go with him," Margaret said.

"Do the best you can. We need him," Kendon said. "I'll be back . . . I'm going to see Harris."

Harris was near the embarkation point. Lines of soldiers were filing into the boats.

"Look over there," he said. "How many do you see?"

"I don't know. Six hundred?"

"There are eleven hundred men still to embark. I'm pretty sure that sometime during the night the Germans will force the perimeter. We've got to have them out by then."

"If they can keep Goodman going, we'll do it!"

"They've *got* to! I've got half a dozen nationalities here. British. Indian. South African. Rhodesian. Each commander wants *all* his men out—and that means the badly wounded, too. They've been round me like dogs all day. Each claims his men are the most important. Each says if they can't be got out, their morale will go to hell. Not only that, but there'll be questions at home which will affect replacements. I was going to leave the really bad cases for the Germans to look after. Much the better way. Now I can't. So they're going to pile up on the far shore of the lake with no transport. We can't push the bloody train *up* the gradient. The Germans will bring their guns up to the edge of the lake here and we'll be sitting in their sights on the far side. What do you think they'll do?"

"Blow us to hell."

"*And* the railway!"

"Colonel!" a voice said urgently.

"Don't interrupt me!" Harris shouted. "I don't care what you do, Kendon. I want that traction engine across on the other side before dark!"

They were carrying Goodman. As they moved up towards the gaol he opened his eyes and said, "The tin . . . I got the tin . . . the tin . . . the tin . . ."

Kendon suddenly realized what he meant. He ran back down the road and searched the area of grass where he had found Goodman. The tin of steam cylinder oil had been flung some distance away, but it was intact.

By the time they reached the gaol Goodman was more coherent. His face had lost all colour and had become waxy. His eyes were dull with pain and shock. He was covered by a heavy blanket and Margaret walked by his side. Every now and then she raised the blanket to inspect the dressing on his stump.

The two soldiers who had carried him put the stretcher down gently. "You'll be all right," Kendon said.

He nodded. "Fine. Yes . . . fine," he whispered. "We'll get the old engine going."

"That's it. We've *got* to get the old engine going. You remember, we'd only filled her with water."

"Fire . . . fire. It takes two hours for the old lady to move."

Little by little the information came. Kendon raised the dampers then lit a fire in the

279

fire-hole. He oiled the worm wheel on the steering and used the precious steam cylinder oil—which had the property of mixing with steam and not rejecting it—to lubricate the piston and valve. He checked the level of water in the shiny brass boiler gauges.

"How long now before she's ready?" he said.

Goodman whispered, "You'll have to wait. She needs at least sixty pounds."

In the darkening room they waited for the needle on the footplate gauge to read sixty pounds pressure per square inch.

Goodman was coming and going like a dying lamp. He had moments of lucidity and moments of derangement and times of unconsciousness. During one of the more lucid moments he told Kendon that the engine used up her water in about an hour and that he'd have to make arrangements for both fuel and water on the far side of the lake. Glad to have something to do, Kendon ran into the town. Harris was organizing the evacuation of the hotel.

"I was just going to send for you. We can't hold out more than a couple of hours," he said. "By dusk we'll only have the centre of the town and the lake shore. We'll be in a pocket. We've got to get that engine of yours out now."

"She's still making up steam."

The Colonel rubbed his haggard cheeks.

"Goodman used bullocks. We might save time by pulling her down to the lake that way."

"You'd never round up bullocks in this shelling."

"What about men?"

"If I ordered anyone from the embarkation points now I'd have a mutiny on my hands."

When Kendon got back to the gaol the gauge was reading fifty pounds pressure.

Goodman's eyes were cloudy with pain. Kendon knelt beside him. "Listen to me. Can she run on fifty?"

Goodman nodded. "Just," he whispered.

"Just is enough."

They lifted him and laid him gently on the footplate of the traction engine. Margaret tried to clamber up beside him but there was no room. "He'll be all right," Kendon said.

He had to open the fire-hole door near Goodman's head to feed more wood into the furnace. Each time he did so the blast of hot air made Goodman gasp, but there was no help for it. The steam pressure gauge was reading between fifty and fifty-five p.s.i., the traction engine was shuddering under the impact of the building pressure, there was a smell of hot oil and burning wood.

"Okay, what do I do?" Kendon yelled.

It was a laborious process. Each question was shouted, each instruction delivered softly so that much of the time he had to bend to hear what Goodman was saying. What made the whole thing possible was the simplicity of the engine itself. Kendon had been around railways long enough to know more or less how locomotives operated. The steam traction engine was built on the same principles.

He was anxious to move off, but even in his extreme state Goodman's concern for what had become in his mind *his* engine checked him and he had to spend some moments with the cylinder taps and the regulator partially open to let out steam that had condensed into water before the metal had heated up sufficiently.

Finally he said, "We've got pure steam."

The engine had originally been pushed through the broken doorway backwards, now all he had to do was engage the larger of the two cogs which gave him top gear. The trembling and shuddering increased. The engine ground forward.

Clanking and juddering it moved into the compound at a steady two miles an hour like some strange, prehistoric animal from the East African bush. To Kendon at the steering handle the movement was remorseless. The massive piece of machinery seemed to be rushing along. There were no brakes so he eased the regulator to the closed position. The traction engine slowed down almost to a stop. He opened it again. The engine picked up momentum. He was in charge, not the machine. He bent and shouted to Goodman, "We've made it!" But Goodman's eyes were closed. The bottom of his blanket was saturated with blood and Kendon realized that when they had picked him up the clamp on his leg must have been dislodged. Had Goodman known? Had he felt the clamp fall away? Had he decided to say nothing? Kendon would never know.

# 15

COLONEL HARRIS had given dusk as the deadline for the evacuation to be completed, but dusk came and darkness followed and still the lines of men waited at the lake shore. The German shelling had grown more intense as the day waned and there were rumours that they had broken through the perimeter. The rumours were false, at least at first. But the Kisimi perimeter was shrinking. By dusk fighting had already reached the mound of rubble which had once been Patel's shop. On the northern edge of the town the Germans had reached the Kisimi Club and the police barracks.

The rain which had slackened off for much of the afternoon had come down heavily again at 5 p.m. and this had helped the British rearguard. The Germans were trying to move forward, the British were trying to stay put; one army had to move its guns in the mud; the other had only to keep theirs in position. After two hours the Germans had abandoned their heaviest guns. Those two hours were vital for the evacuation. The seriously wounded were all away before dusk. To get them away British troops had been held back, but now, as the light faded, as the bombardment increased, they were once more being loaded in twos and fours and sixes and eights into the fleet of small boats that crossed and recrossed the lake towing loaded rafts behind them. The early ones had crossed in safety but now the boats themselves were being fired on.

At first the British troops had been resigned. They had queued as they had been ordered to queue, leaning on their rifles, smoking, sometimes even joking. But then the Germans had renewed the shelling and there was nowhere to take cover. First away had been the walking wounded. Then the Allied troops, the Indians, the South Africans, the Rhodesians, had started embarking. Then the casualties from the hotel were brought down. It wasn't that the British troops resented the dying being brought out, but what they did resent was seeing their Allies get away to the opposite shore while they stood in the Kisimi rain as the German guns plastered the town.

They were angry and frightened and stared anxiously at the bodies which now floated at the lake's edge as evidence of deaths during the crossing. Some bodies were those of the wounded from the hotel. Others were in uniform and the soldiers knew that the Germans had run some of their light guns up to the edge of the lake just outside the town.

It was on to this scene, at dusk, that Kendon burst. The traction engine came down the road, tilting and crashing as it hit the pockmarked surface, rocking and clanking and hissing. At first the men fell back as though the machine heralded the German break-through. But then Kendon waved to them and blew the steam whistle. Those who had fallen back came forward again. They gazed at the engine. Some were familiar with her. They had seen her standing solidly on her plinth in her gleaming paint and brass. Others knew similar engines. They had seen them in the fields at home ploughing or threshing; they had seen them in the cities rolling asphalt, they had seen them on the roads and docks pulling great loads and they had seen them at fairgrounds. The engine was part of home. Someone answered the steam whistle with a shout of welcome. A moment later the lines of men had begun to cheer. They did not know what the traction engine's function was, or that it had anything to do with them. It was there, it was being driven, as far as they could tell, by a British officer, they liked it, they cheered.

Harris was at the water's edge near the raft. It consisted of two ordinary rafts placed one on top of the other, like a sandwich. The filling consisted of empty forty-four-gallon drums.

"Where's Goodman?" Harris said.

"He's dead."

"So are a lot of other people. D'you think she'll go aboard that?"

"We'll soon know."

Kendon eased the regulator fractionally. The big iron wheels bit into the lake mud. The front wheels mounted the raft. Slowly, inch by inch, she humped herself on to the floating platform. By the time she was fully aboard the raft was almost under water.

"She'll do," Harris said.

A boat with a crew of British soldiers lay off the shore. A rope was made fast to the raft. The soldiers began to pull at the oars. Infinitely slowly the engine began to move towards the opposite shore. Because the raft was now completely submerged it appeared as though it were actually travelling on the surface of the water.

"Good luck!" Harris shouted.

"What about fuel and water on the other side?" called Kendon.

"I've sent instructions to have it ready. Don't wait for us. Get the train going as soon as you can!"

Kendon opened the fire-hole door and began throwing in pieces of wood. He wanted as much steam as he could get by the time they reached the far side.

The lake was dead calm. Long before they reached their destination darkness had closed in. During the half-hour crossing Kendon was aware of heavy firing away to his right. Either the Germans had broken into the town or they were firing on the lake craft. He concentrated on the big engine, feeding the fire with wood as he brought the raft ashore.

Robertson was waiting for him. He climbed up on the footplate and held out his hand. "Congratulations," he said. As he spoke they heard the scream of a shell overhead. The Germans had at last managed to bring their heavy guns to the Kisimi shore.

The coaches stood ready. The wounded were packed even tighter than they had been at the hotel. Kendon saw Margaret inside through a lighted window, then the doctor who had kept Goodman alive ran towards him and said, "We're short of drinking water!"

"There's water on the Escarpment."

Another shell screamed overhead and exploded in the bush.

Robertson said, "What about Harris? What about the troops?"

"He said not to wait."

"We can't abandon him!"

"Those were his orders. Anyway, we can't move immediately. She needs water and fuel."

The landing stage was lit garishly by flares and in the shadows he could make out the dark faces and white eyes of the frightened Madrassis who had pushed the coaches and rowed the boats and carried the stretchers. He hoped they would all get medals.

Single shells came over at intervals. Robertson said, "How long will you be?"

"I don't know. We'll have to fill her by hand."

"As soon as you're ready, we'll go. I want all lights doused except for one at the water's edge."

The lights were put out, silence closed in like fog. A single flare burned near the water and was reflected in the dark planes of its surface. Boats carrying the troops began to arrive in a dribble. Some were badly shocked. One of them told Kendon the Germans had forced the head of the main street and the troops had embarked under machine-gun fire.

A shell burst at the landing stage just as a small raft was being poled in. The mirror disintegrated and when Kendon next looked six bodies were floating face down in the water. He turned away and busied himself at the machine. He found he had not become hardened to sudden death.

With the help of half a dozen soldiers he refilled the boiler and the tender. Each pint of water had to be carried from the lake. It took a long time to replace two hundred gallons. Then he loaded up with cut wood. There was a lull in the shelling but at one o'clock it was redoubled and he did not have to be told that the Germans had succeeded in getting a second and perhaps even a third heavy gun to the lake shore.

It rained on and off during the night and soon the area around the landing stage was a quagmire. By two o'clock he had pressure in the boiler up to 180 p.s.i. Several shells had fallen close to the coaches and Robertson was terrified that the tracks themselves might be hit.

"We can't wait any longer," he said. "I'll have the cable made fast."

Kendon brought the traction engine up the slight slope and stopped next to the railway track just ahead of the leading coach. A cable was passed around the couplings of the coach and fastened to the rear of the engine. A dozen Madrassis with torches waited to light the way. The weary troops had climbed onto the roofs of the coaches and were lying down, oblivious of the rain.

"Come on!" Robertson shouted.

Kendon pulled gently on the regulator lever. The engine took up the slack of the cable, it pulled taut. But the coaches did not move. Instead, the huge back wheels of the traction engine began to turn slowly and helplessly in the mud.

He had never experienced anything like that night. Later he could remember the rain and the mud; the cries of the wounded. He would remember the traction engine's wheels spinning. He could remember helping to cut down trees to lay beneath the wheels, and the efforts to push the engine forward by troops who had already given up. He could recall the thud and crash of shells and the sweat that drenched him when the rain was not falling. He could even remember Harris being carried ashore with a bullet in his lung.

In the midst of it all Margaret brought him a cup of tea. It was a half-pint mug and the tea was the colour of rusty water. They moved to the rear of the train and sat on the steps on the sheltered side of a coach. She watched him gulp at the tea and then gave him a cigarette.

"I wish we had a bottle of whisky," she said, leaning her head against his shoulder.

"Even though we're in your other world?"

She shook her head. "They've merged. Ever since this morning when you came to the hotel I knew I couldn't separate the two any longer."

He held her hand and she raised it to her cheek. "When Jeff died and I saw how upset mother was I swore I'd never become so involved with someone that I'd suffer like that. I suppose that's why I stayed with father. If I'd really wanted to I'd have gone. I wanted you, but I knew there was a chance you'd be killed or wounded, so I created my two worlds."

"And now?"

"When the bombardment started we began to get civilians into the hospital. Even nurses were hit. I realized then there was only one world and I'd better start living in it."

He finished his tea and gave her back the mug.

"What about your father?" he said.

"I don't know."

Kendon was silent for a moment, then he said, "I hated him at first."

"Why?"

"For not being the man I thought he was." He told her about his childhood illness and how he had come to read Storey's book, he told her about the friction between them when Storey first came to the camp, the temptation to get rid of him, his disgust at the death of the Nandi tribesmen.

Margaret listened silently. Then she said, "Do you still hate him?"

"No. I think we've both changed; changed each other in a way. The waterhole was the worst thing, yet you can't really blame him. He's come to feel that it's *his* war; he wants to be involved. That was the only thing he could think of. It's the same with the railway; he's become involved in that now, he's part of it. Perhaps that's all he needed; to become part of something again."

"Stop it!" she said and she was crying. "I've made up my mind. I'm not going back to him."

"Of course you're not."

"But what will happen to him?"

"We'll work something out."

By dawn he was able to see the worst. The plain ahead glistened with water. Robertson, who had been overseeing the cutting of brush, came up and said, "Harris died a few minutes ago."

Kendon had known Harris for less than three days and in that time he had grown to respect him. Yet now, hearing of his death, he found he had little emotion left. Physically, he was almost beaten. But not quite. After a moment he said, "We'll have to pull each coach out individually. We'll have to yoke the men like bullocks."

"Half the wounded will be dead by the time we get the first coach to the Scarp," Robertson said.

"Good God, what a mess!"

Kendon looked around and saw Brent. He

stood there, squat and arrogant, his clothes neat, his leather polished, his brass shining. By contrast Kendon and Robertson were streaked with mud, their clothes stained and filthy. Behind Brent stood Sergeant Miller and behind him several *askaris*. All were neat.

"Harris is dead," Brent said.

"I know."

"I shall take command of you from here."

Robertson said, "I am the senior British officer. I shall make the decisions."

"My orders were from the Colonel, just before he died."

"I don't believe you," Robertson said. He looked old and frail.

"That is a matter for you to decide, sir," Brent said.

"For Christ's sake!" Kendon said. "It doesn't matter who's in charge if we can't get the engine moving!"

"Permission to speak, sir," Miller said.

"What is it, Sergeant?"

"If they was to put the spuds on her she'd pull out all right."

"Spuds?"

"Them iron cleats in the front, sir."

The heavy metal cleats were stored in a pan fitted to the front axle. They could be bolted on to the great rear driving wheels through special holes.

Kendon felt a surge of energy. "You're a genius, Miller!"

"My father was a driver, sir."

As they fixed the spuds Kendon said, "What's happened to von Holbach?"

"No sign of him for hours," Brent said. "Probably slipped across the lake to join the Hun on the other side. Anyway, Storey's there with the rest of my men. Ready? I'll lead the way."

"Just one moment!" Robertson said. But Brent ignored him and started shouting his orders. It was their affair, Kendon thought, and eased the regulator. The wheels turned, slipped, then gripped. The traction engine moved slowly forward, towing the coaches on the railway line.

Out in front marched Brent and his small company. They looked very smart in the early light, especially Brent, whose stride exactly matched the pattern of sleepers and whose speed gradually carried him farther and farther out in front.

At the same time that Kendon and his engine were crossing the lake the young lion emerged from the cave. It had gone there after killing Karim Ram. Its leg did not throb so painfully now but it was permanently affected, which meant that the animal would never again have the speed or agility to kill its natural prey and would remain a man-eater or a carrion-eater all its life. It came stealthily towards the construction camp on the side of the Escarpment. This was a different world from the mud and chaos of Kisimi and the lake-side. The coolies slept in peace. Their task was over, the line was built, the war was not their affair. They still lived in their *bomas* but had grown careless and some thorn walls had become ragged where branches had been pulled out for cooking fires.

Jemadar Ragbir Singh was asleep in one of the tents with two other Jemadars when the lion forced a weak point in their *boma*. He came to the flap and pushed it gently. The three sleeping figures were on the far side of the tent. The lion moved silently into the tent, picked up one of the sleepers by the shoulder and began to back out. The man let out a terrified shriek. Jemadar Singh came awake instantly and the first thing he thought was that the very essence of everything he had feared in daemonology was here in his tent.

"Shaitan! Shaitan!" he shrieked. "Devil! Devil!" Totally panic-stricken, he grabbed his *lathi* and began to strike left and right, up and down and in all directions. One of the first blows caught the third sleeper, who also gave a terrified yell.

The lion, still carrying his prey, had backed to the opening and turned to leave, but the opening was too small for both figures. The lion became confused and hurled its weight at the canvas walls. As it did so one of the Jemadar's whirling blows caught it precisely on the wound in its leg. Pain shot up the nerves and blossomed in the animal's brain. With a roar it dropped the man, clawed its way through the opening and forced a second passage through the *boma*. The pain was great but short-lived. Until it subsided, the lion was moving without aim, but he found the railway track and kept to it. The track began to climb. It was unfamiliar territory but the animal kept on; the instinct which had pulled him towards the safety of the cave now pushed him farther and farther from the area of disaster. By dawn he was lying up in the heavy timber near the top of the Escarpment. He was very hungry.

Colonel Storey was also lying near the top of the Escarpment. He was watching, through the telescopic sight of his rifle, the preparations for bringing the wounded up Gradient B. He could hear the chuffing of the steam winch. A carrier began the ascent. It came out of the pit and started up the slope and he saw that it was not carrying a truck. There was only one figure on it and he assumed this to be Kendon.

The Colonel had spent the previous day and two nights in the open. In his youth, even in his middle age, such an event would have been but one of a number, indistinguishable from the next. He had never been a man who worried about comfort, had always been able to sleep rough. But the last time he had been exposed to tropical rain on an exposed hillside, the last time he had slept rough, the last time he had gone without food for nearly thirty-six hours, had been ten years ago, before he had come to Kisimi. Ten years ago he had been as tough as tanned eland skin.

Now he was stiff and his hip pained him. The continuous wettings he had received had brought on a touch of malaria. He was also somewhat more than half-drunk. Cigar had brought him a bottle of whisky late the previous day and there was slightly less than a quarter left. Images were crowding into his mind: the house on the Rufiji, his wife, Margaret, Jeff. They were all there. But shadowy. He sipped the whisky, husbanding it. He thought of the game park; the Jeffrey Storey National Park. He knew there would be no park. The Germans would take the land, or if they didn't, it would be occupied by settlers who would come to Africa after the war. He didn't seem to care any longer.

The empty carrier had reached the Mid-Level and Kendon stepped off. Storey watched him, through the telescopic sight, wave to those below. Another carrier emerged, this time carrying a truck of wounded, and began the ascent. Storey lowered the rifle and looked around the Escarpment on either side of the tracks. Nothing moved. Brent appeared to have been right, the Germans had vanished. Earlier Storey had put himself into von Holbach's position and decided the German was not a man to give up easily. When Brent had made a reconnaissance of the Escarpment, had found nothing and decided to take his men down, Storey had made up his mind to stay. Now it appeared he had exhausted himself and brought on an attack of fever for no reason.

And the fever brought back the picture that he had tried so hard to erase, or if not to erase, at least to obscure; the picture that was now clearer to him than his son's face: the black figure lying on the floor of the tent dying under his very eyes. He had seen death many times, why was this so particular? Having brought the image back into clear focus his mind reproduced von Holbach's searing phrase: "You killed a dozen Nandi. Congratulations!"

It was then he had sent Cigar for the whisky.

He drank, careless of the amount left. The malaria was making him dizzy and the whisky helped to clear his mind.

The carriers were moving on steadily to the Mid-Level now. Kendon searched the slope for Storey. At first when he didn't find him, he assumed him to be well hidden. But then he had questioned one of the *askaris* and learnt that they hadn't seen a German for more than twenty hours. He began to search with more haste. He had almost reached the summit when he heard the chink of bottle on rock. He looked down at Storey. He felt a sudden relief. "I'm glad I found you. Thought you might be hurt."

Storey laughed. "I'm used to roughing it." His face was flushed and his speech blurred. "I watched you," he said. "Marvellous. Well done. The old engine coming across the plain pulling those coaches. Grand sight."

"We couldn't have done it without you. It was your inspiration."

"Rubbish!" But Kendon could see he had been touched and he felt a surge of affection for the old man. There was something indomitable about Storey.

"Is Margaret safe?"

"That's the main reason I came to find you. I knew you'd be worried. Yes, she's safe. We . . . that is, Margaret and I . . ." He stopped. Storey was looking past him and he knew this was not the time.

"Thank God!" Storey said.

"She's coming up now in one of the coaches."

"I'll stay and see her safely up."

"You've seen nothing else? I mean of the enemy."

"Not a thing."

Kendon lifted field-glasses from the rock

302

and swept the side of the Escarpment. "I'll send my Jemadar to give you a hand," he said, and continued up the slope. A crowd of coolies stood on the top of the Escarpment.

Storey watched him go. The corners of his mouth turned down. There was a time when he could have run up and down this slope all day. He had needed no Jemadars to help him then.

There were a good two inches in the bottom of the bottle and he drained it. He tried to push himself to his feet but his head began to swim and, half-fainting, he collapsed into his grassy den with his back to a rock. For some minutes he lay with his eyes closed, breathing in small rapid breaths. The fever increased in intensity and he was hot and cold by turns. His mind began to be affected. In his semi-coma he saw again the face of the dying Nandi, then it was replaced by that of young Kruger, thin and wasted by malaria, whom he had left in his blankets while he walked seven hundred miles for help. That face became Jeff's as he was dying of septicaemia, then his wife's, worn and accusing, and Margaret's face and Kendon's face . . .

His eyes opened and for a second he did not know where he was. Then memory returned.

He pushed himself to his original position and looked down the Escarpment. The funicular on Gradient A was coming into action. A coach was slowly climbing the slope. Soldiers clung to the roof and sides. What if Margaret was in this one? What would he say to her?

He had wanted something to show her after what had happened that night at home—he could not think of the Indian shop-keeper without a deep sense of shame—but there was nothing.

Always before, when he had needed something badly, his rifle had got it for him. But not now. Something had gone wrong inside him. He could no longer pull the trigger.

It was because of Margaret he had stayed on the mountainside in the rain. He had stayed hoping that something, anything, might give him a chance to . . . what?

His brain was too fuddled for clear thinking. All he did know was that nothing had happened, no chance had offered.

More from force of habit than anything else, he raised the rifle and looked through the telescopic sight. A coach was still coming steadily up Gradient A and now he could see that Brent was marching some twenty paces ahead of it, with ramrod back, aware that he had a good audience.

Storey raised the rifle to the top of the Escarpment and let the barrel travel down the line. He kept his eye to the sight. There was nothing. Not a th . . .

It was not so much that he had seen anything as a feeling that his eyes had travelled over a fault in the landscape, something artificial.

He aimed up the slope and brought the barrel down again. There it was. A brownish lump. He kept the sight very still. The lump moved. The movement was only of the slightest, but it gave shape and form.

"Christ!" he whispered. It was von Holbach.

The German was working with a fuse. The package of dynamite on the fish plate was visible through the sight once he knew where to look. Von Holbach must have been hiding behind a pile of cut wood and had crawled to the track on his belly.

There were two carriers on Gradient B and the coach on Gradient A. The coach on Gradient A, led by Brent, was within a hundred feet of the dynamite. Storey could see the complete disaster. Von Holbach would wait until the coach on the funicular was within a preplanned number of yards and then he would light the quick-burning fuse. The charge would blow the coach backwards down the slope on to the waiting coaches below.

The cross-hairs of the sight met on von Holbach's head. Storey's finger was on the trigger. But he couldn't squeeze. It was as though his arm muscles had locked.

"Shoot!" he whispered. "Shoot!"

Then he smelled the lion and knew it was somewhere above him. He felt ice cold. Every nerve in his body screamed at him to turn. But Margaret was in the coach. Kendon had said so. He forced himself to keep his eye clamped to the telescopic sight. He dragged on the trigger. It began to move. He pulled with all his strength.

He heard the shot, and that was all he heard, for the lion was already in mid-spring.

Kendon had been standing high up on the slope watching the coach through his binoculars when he had seen von Holbach. He started to race down the slope. He was about one-hundred-and-eighty yards from the dynamite. He let his body go loose as he sprang down like an antelope. But he had not gone far when he knew he was not going to make it. The coach was slowly approaching the charge. Von Holbach was crouched next to the track, immobile, waiting for the precise moment. Then Kendon heard the rifle crack and saw the bullet bring up dust to von Holbach's left. The German looked around, frightened, then he lit the fuse and ducked behind the wood-pile.

Kendon saw Brent marching in front of the coach. He shouted but Brent did not seem to hear. His head was high, his eyes fixed on the top of the Escarpment where the crowd was standing. Kendon shouted again.

Brent was almost on top of the dynamite when it blew. Bits of sleeper, earth, steel and bits of Captain Brent all shot into the sky.

The charge had gone off too soon. The force of its blast lifted the coach but it came down with its wheels across the track. For a second Kendon thought it was going to roll, but the wheels held. He ran down to it.

The lion pulled the body into deep cover and stayed with it all day. In the late afternoon the noise of the winch and the funicular began again. The lion did not move. Later still it heard voices near the place where Storey had been. It did not move.

Long after full darkness had come to the Escarpment, long after the noise of humans had dispersed into the East African night, long after the lion felt everything to be safe, it crossed the rim of the Escarpment and dropped down into the valley on the far side, passing the sleeping camps. It was leaving the area and would not come back. It loped along the railbed. In the early hours of the morning it drank from a rainwater pool between two sleepers, then it went on, travelling slowly, always keeping to the railway, the source of food.

### THE END

# MYSTERY TITLES
## *in the*
## Ulverscroft Large Print Series

| | |
|---|---|
| Henrietta Who? | *Catherine Aird* |
| Slight Mourning | *Catherine Aird* |
| The China Governess | *Margery Allingham* |
| Coroner's Pidgin | *Margery Allingham* |
| Crime at Black Dudley | *Margery Allingham* |
| Look to the Lady | *Margery Allingham* |
| More Work for the Undertaker | |
| | *Margery Allingham* |
| Death in the Channel | *J. R. L. Anderson* |
| Death in the City | *J. R. L. Anderson* |
| Death on the Rocks | *J. R. L. Anderson* |
| A Sprig of Sea Lavender | *J. R. L. Anderson* |
| Death of a Poison-Tongue | *Josephine Bell* |
| Murder Adrift | *George Bellairs* |
| Strangers Among the Dead | *George Bellairs* |
| The Case of the Abominable Snowman | |
| | *Nicholas Blake* |
| The Widow's Cruise | *Nicholas Blake* |
| The Brides of Friedberg | *Gwendoline Butler* |
| Murder By Proxy | *Harry Carmichael* |
| Post Mortem | *Harry Carmichael* |
| Suicide Clause | *Harry Carmichael* |
| After the Funeral | *Agatha Christie* |
| The Body in the Library | *Agatha Christie* |

| | |
|---|---|
| A Caribbean Mystery | *Agatha Christie* |
| Curtain | *Agatha Christie* |
| The Hound of Death | *Agatha Christie* |
| The Labours of Hercules | *Agatha Christie* |
| Murder on the Orient Express | |
| | *Agatha Christie* |
| The Mystery of the Blue Train | |
| | *Agatha Christie* |
| Parker Pyne Investigates | *Agatha Christie* |
| Peril at End House | *Agatha Christie* |
| Sleeping Murder | *Agatha Christie* |
| Sparkling Cyanide | *Agatha Christie* |
| They Came to Baghdad | *Agatha Christie* |
| Third Girl | *Agatha Christie* |
| The Thirteen Problems | *Agatha Christie* |
| The Black Spiders | *John Creasey* |
| Death in the Trees | *John Creasey* |
| The Mark of the Crescent | *John Creasey* |
| Quarrel with Murder | *John Creasey* |
| Two for Inspector West | *John Creasey* |
| His Last Bow | *Sir Arthur Conan Doyle* |
| The Valley of Fear | *Sir Arthur Conan Doyle* |
| Dead to the World | *Francis Durbridge* |
| My Wife Melissa | *Francis Durbridge* |
| Alive and Dead | *Elizabeth Ferrars* |
| Breath of Suspicion | *Elizabeth Ferrars* |
| Drowned Rat | *Elizabeth Ferrars* |
| Foot in the Grave | *Elizabeth Ferrars* |